A Lady Most Alluring

A GRIMM REGENCY TALE

AMY NEWBOLD

For Greg—*without you, this book would not exist.*

A LADY MOST ALLURING

Cecilia escaped out the door of the cottage and hurried toward the forest that bordered Gillingham Park. The grass was damp from last night's rain and her shoes were wet, but she paid no mind. She had to escape the constant worry of her mother as they settled into their new home. Mama missed London and would have a hard time adjusting to life in the country, but she had no such concerns for herself. A bird called from the grove, and Cecilia was eager to see if she could identify it.

"Cecilia! Come back here this instant!" Mama called.

With a sigh, Cecilia turned back toward the cottage. The bird would have to wait. They had arrived a week ago, and since that time, Mama had been in a flurry of unpacking and organizing their belongings. She supervised cleaning the cottage until it sparkled. With limited staff, Cecilia and her older sister, Miriam, had been called upon to help. "We may have to economize," Mama said, "but that doesn't mean we can't be tidy."

Cecilia wished again that her mother would abandon her mourning clothes. Her refusal to do so would make social engagements awkward in this new area. A full year had passed since Papa died, and Mama still wore the colors of half-mourning—deep grays and dull purples.

"What do you need, Mama?"

Mrs. Barnet gripped Cecilia's hand and pulled her inside. "It isn't fitting for you to run to the woods at this time of day. You'll ruin your shoes and your complexion. Come inside with your sister. Now that we're settled, we may finally spend a civilized afternoon in the parlor."

"Yes, Mama." The parlor was stuffy, and Cecilia groaned at the thought of spending an afternoon inside. She took a seat where she had a view of the main house. Gillingham Park sat on a hill, grand and imposing. It was owned by the Colbournes and Cecilia had yet to make their acquaintance. Their steward had come to give them the keys to the cottage and had shown them around.

Cecilia was, of course, grateful to have a place to live. Mr. Colbourne was a friend of Mama's brother and had taken pity on them when he learned they were losing their London home. Upon Mr. Barnet's death, the inheritance passed to Mr. Darrowby, Cecilia's cousin. It had taken Darrowby months to make arrangements to leave India and return to London, but at long last, he arrived to claim his inheritance and the Barnet women bid farewell to their home.

Cecilia picked up her embroidery while Miriam read in a chair opposite her. She liked keeping her hands busy, and regretted they'd had to leave behind the pianoforte. Music occupied many of her afternoons when they'd lived in London, and she missed it.

"I am certain we will soon receive an invitation to go calling," Mrs. Barnet said, although she sounded anything but certain. "Perhaps I will find a suitable family to whom we ourselves could extend an invitation. With your father gone, rest his soul, it is more important than ever to establish ourselves in this neighborhood and find suitable matches for you girls."

Suitable match. That was the least of Cecilia's concern right now. Her first season in London had ended in a catastrophe that she hoped was now behind her. Last season, the family was in mourning for her father and did not participate in the balls and social events.

Miriam set her book down in her lap. "We shall be forgotten here. Even if we were still in London, without Papa no one would remember us now." Her lips formed a childish pout in stark contrast to the elegant tilt of her head.

Cecelia, tendrils of light brown hair curled about her face, did not look up from her embroidery. "We've only been here a short time. We'll make connections soon enough. Be patient."

"Easy for you to say," Miriam replied, her golden hair neatly coiled and pinned behind her head. "You prefer the company of birds and squirrels to the company of people."

It was true. Cecilia was thrilled by the number of birds and creatures she'd encountered on the one morning walk she'd managed since they arrived. Gillingham Park was filled with species she longed to identify. In London, there were places and people from whom she could seek such knowledge, but she was not in London. And if she were in London, she would not be seeing the variety of birds she found here. It was a conundrum.

Cecelia smiled affectionately at her older sister. "I am sure once it is known that three helpless women have settled here, someone will take pity on us and have us to tea. And once they meet you, dearest, I am sure they will spread the word that a kind, charming young lady is available to meet eligible bachelors in the area."

Miriam paced the room. "If there are any eligible bachelors," she said. "I am beginning to think this part of the country is uninhabited!"

"Well, I shan't mind a break from society," Cecelia said. "Even if there is but one eligible bachelor around, you may have him. I will remain here as a companion for Mama the rest of my days."

"You must socialize here, Cecilia," Miriam said. "You must not let that one little incident interfere with your future."

Cecilia gave her a grateful smile. But Miriam must be the priority. If Miriam were to make a good match here, it would secure her place in society and provide additional stability for their mother.

"Girls," Mama said, her attention drawn to the windows. A rider was coming down the lane at a brisk pace. The rider halted once he reached the house and dismounted. His footsteps crunched on the gravel as he made his way to the front door.

Miriam hurried to her chair. Tucking her dress beneath her, she sat, straight-backed, and faced the parlor door with anticipation.

Meanwhile, Cecilia continued on with her embroidery without so much as an upward glance. Whoever had come to call, it was not her concern. Mrs. Barnet moved away from the window and took a seat.

The butler answered the door and he and the rider exchanged words. The door closed, and footsteps once again crunched across the gravel. Within moments, they saw the horse and rider trotting away. Whomever it was, the caller had not come in for a visit. Miriam slumped back in her chair, letting out a sigh of frustration.

A knock came at the parlor door.

"Yes, Samuels," Mrs. Barnet said.

The butler entered the room with an envelope in his gloved hand. He gave it to Mrs. Barnet. She accepted the envelope and excused him with a polite thank you. Once he left the room, she turned the envelope over and over in her hand.

"Aren't you going to open it, Mama?" Miriam asked.

"Yes, of course." She slit open the envelope and pulled out a card.

"It's an invitation to dine at Gillingham Park the evening after next," she said.

"Oh, whatever shall I wear?" Miriam asked, then paused. "We are going, aren't we?"

"Yes, we will attend," Mrs. Barnet said, looking pointedly at Cecilia. "All of us. Although I must remind you, Cecilia, to not make a scene."

Cecilia frowned. Mama never failed to remind her not to draw attention to herself. She mustn't talk too much or say the wrong thing. She must dress appropriately, but must not outshine anyone else in the room. She knew all the rules and did her best to follow them, but making herself invisible during social engagements was taxing. She'd prefer not to go.

"Perhaps it would make sense for me to remain here, Mama. It would be easier for you and for Miriam if I am not there to make a mess of things. She is the priority now and should have all the new dresses and ribbons we can afford. I'm not certain I have anything to wear."

"It isn't a ball or formal occasion, Cecilia. Our dresses will be adequate, and although you are correct, we will be prioritizing new clothing for Miriam, that does not give you an excuse to become a recluse," Mrs. Barnet said.

Cecilia sighed. She dreaded making small talk all evening and having to perform after dinner. The pianoforte was the one area where she could shine, but Mama always encouraged her to play below her capabilities. And now, without an instrument to practice on anymore, her skills would diminish. Perhaps she could find a chair in a dim corner and pass the evening unnoticed. But she wondered if even that would be enough to make Mama happy.

Miriam went to Mama and clasped her hands. "Please may we go to the village and buy ribbons? I need new ones for my hat, and my last season's gown could use a bit of lace to refresh it. Cecilia is handy with a needle. You'll help me, won't you Sissy?"

The nickname made Cecilia smile. Miriam's excitement

was contagious, and she would do anything for her older sister. "Of course I'll help," she said.

"Girls, you bring me joy. I'm sure we can spare the expense. You must go to the village and buy ribbons," Mama said.

"We shall go tomorrow. Oh, Sissy, won't that be an adventure?" Miriam exclaimed.

"Yes," Cecilia said. She was eager to explore their new surroundings.

CHAPTER TWO

$\mathscr{B}$enedict Lockhart paced back and forth in the library of Oakwood Manor. He had already spoken with the steward, taken care of his correspondence, and reviewed the accounts. The day stretched before him, endless hours with nothing to fill them. In London, he could visit his club, spend time with his friends, and anticipate multiple events to fill his evenings: dinners, theater, musical performances, balls, and more.

"Pardon me, Mr. Lockhart, but Mrs. Lockhart requests your company in the dining room."

"Of course," he replied. "Thank you."

Mother was awake and having a late breakfast. Benedict had accompanied her to the country at his father's request. She needed to convalesce and thought the best place to restore her health was Oakwood Manor. Benedict took his charge seriously, not only because the sooner Mother was well, the sooner he could return to London, but also because he was quite fond of her.

"Good morning," he greeted her as he entered the dining hall. She sat alone at the long table wearing a beige dressing gown. Her face was pale beneath her cap, but her smile was warm and welcoming.

"Keep an old woman company," she said, gesturing at a chair. "I suppose you ate already?"

"Hours ago," he said. "While you were getting your beauty sleep."

She patted his hand. "You are such a tease. What have you been busy with this morning while I rested?"

Benedict filled her in on his morning activities while she ate. He hid his worry as she took delicate bites and left much of the breakfast untouched.

"It must be tedious for you here," she said. "We shall plan a social event to liven things up for you. A ball, I think. Yes, a masquerade ball. I'll invite your sister to help me plan it. It shall be the event of the summer. Late August would be best, before people think of returning to London. What do you say?"

The last thing Benedict wanted was to have a masquerade ball, but if it would make his mother happy, he would participate. Having something to look forward to might improve her health.

"You haven't yet found a young lady to wed in London but there will be new prospects for you here," she continued.

He protested, but she shushed him. "It's time for you to find a wife, Benedict. I am not getting any younger, and I'd love to see you settled. Oakwood Manor would be the perfect place for you to bring a bride and to raise my grandchildren."

"But you know I love London, Mother. I'd prefer a young lady who also loves the city. And I believe it's much too early to be discussing grandchildren."

"Don't wait too long, Benedict. Life is better in the company of someone that you respect and admire." Mrs. Lockhart wiped the beads of sweat from her face with her handkerchief. She already seemed tired enough to return to her bed.

"Are you feeling ill, Mother? Shall I call your maid?" Benedict asked.

"Yes, thank you," she said. "I am poor company this morning. Perhaps I will be strong enough to go outdoors into the garden later this afternoon. You may accompany me, and we shall have tea."

"I'd be happy to," he said, ringing for her ladies' maid. He stayed with her until her maid arrived to help her back to her room. What if her condition didn't improve? He wondered if he should contact the local doctor. If Father were here, he would know what to do. But he wasn't here, and Benedict was in charge.

Father was testing him, making sure he was prepared to receive his inheritance one day. Benedict did not feel up to the task. Father had always run everything to perfection, and now Benedict feared getting things wrong.

He wandered to the library and perused the shelves. He could pass the afternoon reading, but the prospect did not appeal to him. A knock at the door interrupted his thoughts.

"Come in," he said.

"Mr. Colbourne, sir," said the butler.

Benedict rushed over to greet his friend. "Duncan, it's good to see you." The two had spent many hours together roaming their respective properties while growing up. They'd also found more than their share of trouble. Duncan rarely visited London, so most of their time together came during the Lockharts' visits to the countryside.

"You're looking well, but I dare say you need time in the fresh air to shake off that London pallor," Duncan said. He and Benedict were nearly the same height, but the reddish hue of Duncan's hair was in stark contrast to Benedict's dark locks.

Benedict scowled at his friend. "It is not my aim to return to London browned and disheveled. Or with a wife."

Duncan laughed. "A wife? That took an unexpected turn."

Benedict grinned. "Yes, Mother thinks I might find my perfect match here, although I find that unlikely."

"Well, if you and Alice could form an attachment, it would make both of our families very happy," Duncan said.

Alice was Duncan's sister and had often trailed after Benedict and Duncan on their escapades. She and Benedict had decided long ago they had sibling-like affection for one another and not romantic feelings. Despite Mrs. Lockhart's best efforts to encourage Benedict to make a request for her hand, Benedict stuck to his promise to Alice that he would not. They shared a commitment to maintaining their friendship.

"How is Alice?" Benedict asked.

Duncan sat down and propped his long legs up on the desk. "Alice is the same as ever. Elegant, funny, and driving my parents crazy. She's been trying to convince Mother to send her on a European tour. She is certain that her true love will be from somewhere more exotic than England."

Benedict sat across from Duncan. "If she manages to run off to Europe, let me know. I'll follow her to escape the masquerade ball Mother is planning."

Duncan laughed. "If she goes, I'll tell you first, I promise. Mother sent me to invite you and Mrs. Lockhart to dine with us. She is hosting a small party, and we will honor your return as well as welcome our new tenants. I do hope Mrs. Lockhart is well enough to attend."

"I don't know if it will be too much for her," Benedict said. "Although it would brighten her mood to be around your mother."

"You must come and stay for the week then. We have plenty of room. Mrs. Lockhart can convalesce at Gillingham Park as well as she can here at Oakwood Manor. Our mothers will plot our future and you and I shall plot how to avoid their plans," Duncan proposed.

"We should begin plotting now to get a step ahead of them. What if we made a little wager between friends?"

"Regarding our future brides? We shouldn't bet on the ladies," Duncan replied.

"No, not on the ladies. That would be improper. But I wager I can offend all the eligible ladies here and return to London unattached."

"Offend?" Duncan rose to his feet and paced the room. "I don't like the sound of that."

"Not truly offend. I would never do anything to reflect poorly on Mother. But if I am not gracious, if I am terse in my responses, I believe I can put off most of the young ladies here and stop their advances."

"You mean, be yourself? That won't make much of a wager."

Benedict scowled. "I can be gracious."

Duncan traced his finger along the book spines on the shelf. "I will take your wager and bet that you will find the woman of your dreams before Michaelmas. I am certain someone here will capture your attention."

"And when I win?" Benedict asked, sincerely hoping he was back in London well before Michaelmas.

"You'll win your freedom from provincial attachments."

"And if I lose?"

"You'll win your bride," Duncan said. "Either way, I believe you will come out the winner."

The clouds hung low in the sky and a steady rain blurred the view. Miriam's forehead wrinkled as she glared out the window. "It isn't fair that Cousin Darrowby took the carriage along with everything else. We'll never be able to go to the village for ribbons today."

"You know we couldn't keep a carriage and horses and stable hands and a driver. The clouds are growing lighter. The rain may stop by afternoon, and we'll go then," Cecilia said.

Miriam and Cecilia both struggled to pass the time, but eventually the rain became a slight drizzle, and they set out for the village. Cecilia was careful to hold her umbrella in a position that provided the most protection for her dress. She didn't mind the rain, but she didn't want to arrive at the village soaked to the skin. Miriam huddled next to her. They walked along the road, skipping over puddles in a vain attempt to keep their shoes dry.

As they approached the milliner's shop, a team of horses passed by at a rapid pace. Cecilia instinctively stepped nearer the road to shield Miriam from the carriage. The carriage wheels splashed through a puddle, sending a cascade of mud and water over them. Cecilia caught the brunt of it. Even her cheek was covered in the brown muck.

A man gazed out the carriage window at them. His eyes met Cecilia's, and she saw the chiseled cut of his chin, the lock of deep brown hair escaping his hat. The carriage slowed and Cecilia was sure he would stop and offer assistance, or at the very least, apologize. But he did no such thing. To her amazement, he tipped his hat to her and the carriage continued forward.

Cecilia raised her fist at him, though she doubted he could see her. A glob of mud fell from her sleeve and splattered on her already filthy skirt.

"The audacity!" Cecilia stepped forward to run after the carriage, but Miriam's hand on her arm stopped her.

"Don't, Sissy. It will do no good. What's done is done. Besides, Mama would not want you to make a scene. Where's your handkerchief?" Miriam's skirt was spattered but not soaked. Cecilia's dress, on the other hand, was quite drenched and she feared that it would ever come clean.

Rummaging in her reticule, Cecilia failed to find a handkerchief. "I seem to have forgotten to bring one." She glanced after the carriage, now stationed at an establishment up the street, and pulled a face.

"Hold still," Miriam said. She used her sleeve to wipe Cecilia's face. "We'd better head home and soak these clothes before the stains set."

"I can't believe that man was so rude." Cecilia stomped her foot, splashing them again with mud. Miriam shrieked and jumped out of the way.

Cecilia took Miriam's arm, and they headed back toward Gillingham Park. She was beyond frustrated. The longer it took to find ribbons and lace, the less time Cecilia would have to add them to Miriam's hat and dress. Their maid-of-all-work wasn't skilled with a needle, unlike their former ladies' maid in London, and they couldn't afford to hire out the work in town. How she missed being able to go to a dressmaker.

A man on horseback, rain dripping from his coat and hat, pulled to a stop beside them. "Ladies, may I be of assistance to you?"

Cecilia started to tell him no, but he was already dismounting.

"Whatever happened?" he asked, concern filling his brown eyes.

"That carriage drove by and splashed us without even a pause or an apology," Cecilia told him, pointing down the road.

Was she mistaken or did his face fill with recognition when he saw the carriage? "Perhaps the driver didn't see you. Allow me." He pulled a handkerchief from his pocket and offered it to Miriam, even though it was clear that Cecilia needed it more.

"Thank you, Mr...?" Miriam took the handkerchief and dabbed at her face before passing it to Cecilia.

"Colbourne. Duncan Colbourne at your service."

"Why Mr. Colbourne, how kind of you. We are your new tenants, Miriam and Cecilia Barnet."

He tipped his hat to each of them in turn, and his eyes flicked over Cecilia before returning to Miriam. Cecilia cleaned her face the best she could and offered the handkerchief back to him.

He waved it away. "Please keep it. I have others."

Miriam took the handkerchief. "I will see that it is cleaned."

"Do you know whose carriage that is?" Cecilia asked.

Duncan frowned and shook his head. "May I accompany you home?"

Cecilia bit her lip before she could ask him if he intended to take all three of them on horseback. Those were the kinds of things that burst from her mouth unbidden and embarrassed her mother during social functions. Too bad Mama wasn't here to witness her moment of restraint.

"Thank you, but we shall be fine. We are already soaked

through, and the walk is not far," Miriam said. "We shall see you at the dinner party."

Mr. Colbourne bowed before mounting his horse. Cecilia and Miriam made their way back to Gillingham Park.

"I am sorry we weren't able to get any lace," Miriam said.

"I have the bit of lace I've been saving," Cecilia began.

"No. I won't take it. It's the last memento you have of Aunt Cecilia, and I know she'd want you to use it for a special occasion. Perhaps we can take some lace from one of Mama's old dresses."

Cecilia hopped over a mud puddle. It warmed her that Miriam wanted her to keep her lace. It was important to have Miriam appear at her best, but Cecilia was not yet ready to part with the gift from her dear aunt. Besides the lace, her aunt left her a small locket and a pair of pale blue gloves. And despite her protestations about not wanting to socialize, Cecilia had often pictured herself using the lace, gloves, and locket on her own wedding day.

Aunt Cecilia was Mama's favorite sister who had passed away when Cecilia was ten. Prior to her death, she had lived with the Barnets. Never married, Aunt Cecilia always had time for her nieces. Cecilia remembered taking long walks, soaring on a swing hung from a large oak tree in the yard, reading by the fire, and practicing dance steps in the parlor. Days and evenings filled with love and laughter. Cecilia hoped that one day her choices would make her aunt proud. But until then, she would do her best to keep out of trouble and help Miriam succeed.

CHAPTER
FOUR

$\mathcal{B}$enedict rose from his seat in the corner of the coffee house to get Duncan's attention. His friend tilted his head in acknowledgement and made his way over to the table. A boy scurried across the room to bring Duncan a cup of coffee.

"I was surprised to find this place," Benedict said, gesturing around the room. Dark wood paneled the walls and the weak afternoon light from the few windows did little to liven up the place. The room was sparsely populated with men seated at the round tables.

"We are very modern here in the countryside," Duncan replied, a smile spreading across his face. "London does not have an exclusive on entertainment."

"Yes, it is very forward-thinking here," Benedict said, his voice tinged with sarcasm. He flipped idly through the stack of newspapers on the table, choosing one and scanning the contents. With parliament not in session, he was curious to see what filled the paper.

"Anything interesting?" Duncan asked.

"Mrs. Lockhart and her son, Mr. Benedict Lockhart, have taken up residence for the summer at Oakwood Manor. Mr. Lockhart is a gentleman of considerable wealth and will be of interest to the local young ladies."

Duncan coughed and sprayed coffee on the table. He retrieved a napkin and mopped at the mess. "I suppose you have no chance of remaining anonymous now. The invitations will be piling up at your door."

"Mother needs peace and quiet to regain her strength. That shall help me limit my social calendar." Benedict scanned the paper for interesting bits to share with Duncan.

"Our Prince Regent is up to his usual antics, and Lady W—is going through divorce proceedings in court. Oh wait, here's something. 'Miss Anne H. will find her marriage prospects limited after being found unchaperoned with Lord M at Lady Templeton's garden party last week.'"

He thumped the paper onto the table. "I will never understand why a reputable paper would print such drivel."

Duncan sighed. "Another lady's reputation stained by the thoughtless action of a man. The appetite for gossip here is growing. It is one thing I wish stayed in London. Imagine if this happened to Alice."

Benedict shook his head. "Alice's reputation is impeccable as are her manners. She would never be caught in such a situation. But it is most appalling that someone could ruin it all for her in a moment of indiscretion."

"I hope this never happens to her," Duncan said.

Benedict took a sip of coffee and pulled a face. "While I appreciate this coffee shop, the coffee could use some improvement."

"It could indeed," Duncan said. He rubbed his fingertips along the edge of the table and glanced around the room before clearing his throat.

"What is on your mind?" Benedict asked.

"I ran into two young ladies on my way here. They seem to have had a bad encounter with your carriage."

Benedict did not meet Duncan's eyes. "It was very muddy. I could not do anything about it."

"You might have stopped and offered assistance. Or an apology."

Benedict picked up his cup and drank more of the terrible coffee. "That would have accomplished nothing. What was I supposed to do, offer them a ride? Then not only would their clothing be in ruins, but also the inside of my carriage."

"They were quite upset," Duncan said. "Rightfully so."

Benedict drummed the table with his fingers. "An apology would not have helped me win my wager. Word is out," he pointed back to the newspaper, "that I am here. It is in my best interest to be a bit of a rogue. Besides, I did not recognize the ladies and therefore, they are of little consequence to me."

Duncan opened his mouth as if to say something but stopped. He shrugged and leaned back in his chair. "You are off to a good start on your wager. We shall see how well you do once you are in social engagements. You are coming to dinner, are you not?"

Benedict nodded. "Mother has agreed to stay for the week and I am looking forward to it."

A gentleman approached their table, waiting nearby for a pause in their conversation. He was of average height, his hands resting on his substantial waist. He nodded a greeting to Duncan.

"Mr. Fielding, how good to see you," Duncan said. "Allow me to introduce you to my friend, Mr. Benedict Lockhart."

Mr. Fielding turned his attention to Benedict. "It is good to meet you. I have heard much about you since moving here. My family is very eager to make your acquaintance. I shall make sure we extend an invitation to you soon."

Benedict fiddled with his cuffs as Mr. Fielding continued to talk, finding it difficult to concentrate on what the man was saying. He nodded in agreement once or twice and was about to offer a verbal affirmation when something sharp hit his shin. He straightened with a start and caught Duncan giving him a slight shake of the head. Whatever he'd been about to agree to, he got the distinct feeling that Duncan had saved him.

After several minutes, Mr. Fielding excused himself and Benedict leaned across the table. "You kicked me. What was that all about?"

Duncan laughed. "It was a warning. You were about to become attached to one of Mr. Fielding's daughters. Maybe not an engagement, but you were on the verge of agreeing to escort Miss Fielding to several summer functions. And while the Fielding sisters are nice enough, I doubt you wish to be committed to one of them having never met."

"Thank you, my friend, for keeping me from a grave mistake."

Duncan straightened the stack of newspapers and rose from his seat. "You must be careful here. While you have been here many times in the past, never have you been such an eligible marriage prospect. I'll look forward to your visit."

Benedict followed Duncan outside. Scattered clouds drifted across the blue sky and the ground was drying. He instructed the driver to take him back to Oakwood Manor, and as he climbed inside the carriage, he wondered who the young ladies were that had been splashed by the mud. Duncan had not disclosed their identities, which, now that Benedict thought about it, was odd. Were they new also? Or was there some other reason Duncan had withheld the information?

He steadied himself as the carriage hit a bump. No matter. Whoever they were, it was of no interest to him. He would have time enough to seek a bride when he returned to London. Until then, he would enjoy his time with the Colbournes until Mother was fully recovered.

**CHAPTER
FIVE**

When the evening for the dinner party finally arrived, the Barnet women clustered in the cottage doorway looking out at the rain. They were dressed for dinner at Gillingham Park. Mrs. Barnet hesitated.

"Perhaps we should not go, Mama," Cecilia suggested, knowing her mother and sister did not enjoy walking in inclement weather.

"There is no help for it," Mrs. Barnet said, unfurling her umbrella and stepping outside. "We've already accepted the invitation, and we shall hurry along as best we can. Watch your step, girls, and do try to avoid the mud."

They scurried up the drive, sticking to the edges where the gravel was undisturbed by horses and carriages and provided better protection for their shoes and skirts. Even with the umbrellas, they were quite damp when they arrived at the big house.

The butler ushered them inside while another servant collected their umbrellas. Cecilia shed her pelisse and handed it to a waiting maid. It was too warm for the garment, but it had protected her dress from the rain. Her shoes were soaked, which added to her discomfort this evening. She joined her mother and sister as they followed the butler into an elegant parlor where they found a small group of people. She was grateful the gathering was not larger.

"Mrs. Barnet, Miss Barnet, and Miss Cecilia," the butler announced before leaving the room.

Cecilia stood back from her family. She longed to disappear, but her superior height made that impossible. She thought of her father who always encouraged her to focus on the advantages her extra inches gave her. But standing out in a crowd was not, in her opinion, one of those advantages.

A plump woman rushed toward them, her smile warm and welcoming. Her hair was streaked with gray.

"You braved the rain! I am so glad. I'm Mrs. Colbourne, and we are thrilled to have the cottage occupied once again. Please make yourself at home, and we will dine shortly."

If Mrs. Colbourne thought it odd that Mrs. Barnet wore mourning clothes, she did not say anything. For that, Cecilia was grateful. Her mother's appearance made things awkward enough without people commenting on it.

While her mother chatted with Mrs. Colbourne, Cecilia surveyed the room. Draperies hung above the tall windows, and the thick carpet was comfortable beneath her wet shoes. An assortment of chairs and sofas, upholstered in pastel colors, were tastefully arranged around the room. A gentleman joined Mrs. Colbourne, and Cecilia heard him introduced as Mr. Colbourne. The rest of the party was comprised of three gentlemen and two ladies. She recognized Duncan Colbourne. He was talking earnestly to a man who looked to be his age, while a young woman stood off to the side.

Wait. She'd seen that man before. The line of his jaw. The shock of dark hair curving over one eyebrow. As if he felt the weight of her gaze, he turned to look at her. Cecilia froze, certain now that she recognized him. The man from the carriage. He tilted his head toward her and gave her a slight smile.

He was Duncan Colbourne's acquaintance. Perhaps even his friend. That was why Mr. Colbourne seemed insincere when he denied knowing who owned that carriage. Duncan knew and had not been honest with her to protect his friend.

"Miriam, that's the man who splashed us with mud," Cecilia said under her breath.

Miriam squinted and then gripped Cecilia's arm. "It is indeed. Whatever shall we say to him?"

"Leave that to me," Cecilia said.

Miriam did not let go of her arm. "You mustn't make a scene, Sissy. Mama wouldn't want you to."

"I know," she said. She was like a young horse straining at the bit, longing to run free. Longing to tell both Mr. Colbourne and his friend what she thought of them. But she mustn't cause trouble for her family.

When a servant announced that the meal was ready, the group arranged themselves to walk to the dining room. Mr. Colbourne escorted his wife, while the man from the carriage escorted an older woman whom Cecilia guessed was his mother. Mrs. Barnet took the arm of the other older gentleman. Cecilia had already forgotten his name.

"Allow me to accompany you, Miss Barnet. It is a pleasure to see you again. This is my sister, Alice." Mr. Duncan Colbourne offered his arm to Miriam.

And that left Cecilia. She trailed after the group, keenly aware that she was out of place here. She thought of leaving. It wouldn't be a long walk home and she doubted anyone would miss her.

Alice peered over her shoulder and let go of her brother's arm. "Why Miss Cecilia, it will never do to have you unaccompanied. We shall walk in together."

Cecilia was too surprised by the unexpected kindness to formulate a proper response. She continued alongside Alice, who seemed to have no problem bringing up the rear.

"Mother can never seem to put together a party with the right number of ladies to gentlemen no matter how hard she tries. Something always goes wrong. But we are happy to have you in the neighborhood."

"Thank you," Cecilia said. "Who is that man your brother was speaking to?"

"That's Benedict Lockhart. He's Duncan's friend," Alice said. "He's the most eligible man in the neighborhood, but no one has managed to capture his heart yet. I suspect he's holding out for a mythical creature that doesn't exist. And that's Mrs. Lockhart, his mother."

Cecilia saw him lean toward Mrs. Lockhart as she made conversation with him. His shoulders were broad, pulling the fabric of his coat taut. He was tall, tall enough that she wouldn't feel awkward beside him. And his hair was thick and full. If appearances were the only measure of a man, then he would rank near the top of anyone's list.

Once in the dining hall, a footman held her chair for her, and she settled in at the table across from Mr. Lockhart. Good, Cecilia thought. It would give her a chance to confront him about the carriage incident. The bowl of soup set before her smelled wonderful and she was careful not to slurp as she tasted it.

Benedict spoke to Alice, who was seated to his left. Cecilia couldn't help but notice his straight nose, squared jaw, and to her surprise, a dimple in his cheek. He turned his attention to her.

"Have you found Gillingham Park to your liking?"

"Yes, although I had a rather astonishing encounter in the village the other day. A gentleman's carriage splashed me and my sister with mud, ruining one of our dresses, and he showed no remorse."

Mr. Lockhart's face flushed a deep red. He cleared his throat. "While that is most unfortunate, I believe we may both agree that the gentleman was not responsible for the weather or the condition of the road."

"He may not control the weather, but he was well aware of the road condition. And he must have seen us."

"He was not the driver."

"He was not driving," Cecilia conceded, the memory of Mr. Lockhart tipping his hat to her sparking anger. She sat up straighter and squared her shoulders. "But as the person who hired the driver, he had some responsibility and could have taken many different actions, including apologizing to the ladies who were harmed." She set down her spoon, having lost any appetite for the soup course.

Mr. Lockhart was about to respond, an intense gaze in his blue eyes, when the platter of meat arrived before them. He deftly served himself, Alice, and Miriam, who sat at his other side. Cecilia waited for the beef to reach Mr. Colbourne, who sat next to her. He served her and she thanked him, although she never understood why she was not allowed to choose her own cuts of meat at the meal.

"Besides ill-fated walks to the village, have you found other activities to your liking?" Mr. Colbourne asked.

Cecilia was more than happy to have the conversation change. "Oh yes, I much prefer Gillingham Park to London. There are so many birds here. I love waking to birdsong, and I'm longing to identify as many of them as I can," she said.

The words came out louder than she intended and happened to fall during a lapse in the conversations around her. The room was silent as the guests turned to look at her, including Mrs. Barnet who gave her a disapproving glare. Cecilia's cheeks grew warm as she tried to think of something to say. Surely there was nothing wrong with an interest in birds. Although perhaps it was not common. No, her real sin was being noticed at all. Her shoulders slumped.

"I love birds as well," Alice said, filling the void in the conversation. "Perhaps we could go walking one morning and I'll introduce you to the birds of the Park. We have a field guide or two in the library that you are welcome to borrow as well."

As everyone returned to their conversations, Cecilia thanked Alice for her offer. "I'd like that very much," she said.

She focused on her plate, cutting a tender morsel of meat. As she lifted it to her mouth, she found Benedict Lockhart watching her with a bemused look on his face. She looked away, annoyed that he still had not issued an apology. Having to concede that he had not been driving made her feel worse. She glanced up to see Miriam talking to him, but he didn't appear to be listening. His eyes were penetrating, and Cecilia found being on the receiving end of his attention disconcerting. She couldn't read his expression, but felt as if he were taking her measure, and that she was somehow found wanting.

After dinner, the ladies retired to the parlor while the men gathered for drinks in another room. Cecilia chose a seat near the window. She would have ducked behind the draperies if she could. Her mother gave her an approving nod. Miriam was settled near Alice and Mrs. Lockhart. In the candlelight, her face and hair were radiant. Mama and Mrs. Colbourne sat nearby.

With the ladies engaged in conversation, Cecilia let her mind wander. What if Miriam married well and ended up running a household such as this? Perhaps Mama would be able to live with Miriam. With the two of them secure and stable, Cecilia wondered what the future might hold for her. Perhaps she could seek a governess position. London may afford her more opportunities, but she would prefer to be close enough to Miriam that they could visit one another.

Cecilia stifled a yawn. She wondered how much longer they would have to stay, if it was still raining, if they would have to walk home in the dark. Miriam's laugh rose above the conversation, delicate like musical notes. If Mr.

Colbourne and Mr. Lockhart could see her now, Cecilia was sure they would be intrigued, if not completely smitten.

The parlor doors opened, and the men joined them. Mr. Colbourne walked over to his wife and had a brief, quiet conversation.

"We shall have some entertainment," Mrs. Colbourne declared. "Alice, as we are the hosts of this evening, perhaps you would entertain us first with something on the pianoforte. Then Miss Barnet and Miss Cecilia may follow."

Miriam demurely studied her hands in her lap while Mrs. Barnet cleared her throat. Cecilia looked over at her. Would Mama ask her not to play? Instead, Mama pursed her lips in a thin line and gave Cecilia a slight shake of her head. Cecilia did not need help interpreting what her mother meant. Let Miriam shine. Don't take any attention for yourself.

Alice played and sang a familiar tune, encouraging the others to join in. The piece was simple, and her stumbles were covered by the singing. Alice bowed with flare when she finished, causing Mr. Lockhart to reward her with a smile. A smile that showed his dimple. Why did he have to be so handsome?

The guests applauded politely and then waited for Miriam to take her place. At home, Miriam was indifferent to the pianoforte, and Cecilia wondered how well she would play. She winced when Miriam made a mistake. Duncan Colbourne was standing near the instrument, and he gave no notice. Perhaps he was more interested in Miriam herself than he was in how she played. Mr. Lockhart, however, had his eyes on Cecilia. When Miriam finished, Cecilia went to the instrument and took a seat.

"Do you wish to look through the music?" Mrs. Colbourne asked.

"No thank you," she said. She longed to play something

intricate, to let her fingers fly on the keyboard, but after Miriam's rather inept performance, she didn't dare. Mama would not be pleased. Even though she no longer had a pianoforte on which to practice, she was not concerned about losing her skill yet. Cecilia chose a piece she knew by heart. In deference to Mama, she simplified chords and slowed the timing. It took some effort, but she believed Mama would be pleased.

Cecilia finished playing and made her way back to her hidden chair. Mr. Lockhart stepped in front of her and obstructed her path.

"I'd like to hear you play that the way it was intended," he said.

"I don't know what you mean," she said, flustered.

"I believe you played with great restraint," he replied.

"I'm sorry to disappoint you." Cecilia hoped that someone would step in to rescue her from this conversation. Alice and Miriam were talking with Mr. and Mrs. Colbourne. Mrs. Lockhart was seated on a chair.

"Miss Cecilia, what a talent you have." It was the other gentleman, the one whose name she could not remember. His hair was graying at the temples, but his eyes were kind.

"That is gracious of you, sir," she said. "Please excuse me, I must join my mother."

This was not at all how she planned the evening to go—having two men seeking out her attention. Miriam was the one who should be the center of their interest.

"I'd like to leave, Mama. I feel a headache coming on."

"You aren't taking ill, are you?" Mama asked, her voice full of concern.

Cecilia shook her head. "I'm rather tired."

Mama thanked Mrs. Colbourne for the evening.

"Must you leave so soon?" their hostess asked.

"I'm afraid so," Mama said.

"I shall send for the carriage. There is no need for you to walk in the dark when it is raining."

Cecilia was grateful. The carriage was brought, and they hurried out into the rain and scrambled safely inside. No wonder Alice was so kind, Cecilia thought. She took after her mother.

"I would say that evening was a great success," Mrs. Barnet said. "You both comported yourselves well. Especially you, Cecilia."

She had done it. Stayed in the corner. Played poorly enough. Mrs. Barnet was happy with her as long as she stifled herself. Cecilia believed it was worth it. Keeping Mama happy, helping Miriam, it needed to be enough. Maybe someday it would be her turn to shine, but not now. Not yet.

Back at the cottage, she brushed her hair before bed. How had Mr. Lockhart known she wasn't playing as well as she could? Why had he noticed her despite her best efforts to be forgettable? She should still be angry with him over her muddy dress, but his dimple seemed to be getting in the way.

CHAPTER SIX

The dew sparkled on the grass in the morning sun as Benedict and Duncan set out from Gillingham Park for a ride. Benedict had to admit that he enjoyed the quiet of these early morning hours. But he would rather have been in London.

"Why didn't you tell me the ladies my carriage splashed were the dinner guests?" Benedict asked.

"I wanted to see the look on your face," Duncan said.

"Some friend you are." As much as he wanted to look stern, Benedict found himself grinning at Duncan. Perhaps it was the fresh morning air that elevated his mood.

"It was worth it," Duncan said. "How long will you stay in the country this time?"

"Until Mother recovers her health. It would make her happy if I found a bride here, but as we already agreed, I shall scare off all the young ladies of the neighborhood," Benedict replied with an air of confidence. Despite attending countless balls and social events in London, and despite a long string of eligible young ladies pursuing him, he had not been able to meet a woman who could hold his attention for more than one evening. And he couldn't fathom settling down for the rest of his life with someone with whom he couldn't have a decent conversation.

"And did either of the Barnet sisters catch your fancy last evening?" Duncan asked.

Benedict slowed his horse. "Miss Barnet was pleasant, but not memorable, I'm afraid."

"And Miss Cecilia?"

Miss Cecilia indeed, with tendrils of hair escaping the knot at her neck, and with that smattering of freckles across her nose. He shook his head. She seemed rather…unrefined.

"She had adequate skill on the pianoforte. And if I heard correctly, she and Alice share a rather unconventional interest in birds."

Duncan laughed. "Yes, she and Alice did seem to form a connection. Are you certain you are not right for Alice?"

"I am certain. Alice will find the perfect person for her," Benedict said, "and I shall tease her mercilessly about him for the rest of our lives."

"You can't blame a man for trying. It would be perfect if we were not only friends, but also brothers. Why are you reluctant to settle down?"

"I have a fear of being attached to a woman who bores me. Can you imagine spending evenings at home in awkward silence because in the first two months of married life you exhausted all topics of conversation? I want someone who continues to surprise me. Or who at least can be interesting."

"If you married Miss Cecilia, she could play music while the two of you didn't speak after your evening meal," Duncan teased. "Rumor has it you are looking for a bride. Perhaps you need to show interest in someone, otherwise women will be flocking after you."

Benedict grunted. "I would never play with a lady's feelings like that, Duncan. I may be a bit of a rogue, but I am also somewhat of a gentleman."

Benedict urged his horse into a gallop. Duncan followed and they raced across an open field, with Benedict gaining a small lead before they reined the horses back to a walk. It wouldn't do to bring the animals back hot and breathing hard.

"I beat you in the race, my friend, and I'll win our wager as well," Benedict said.

"We'll see. I can imagine a young lady capturing your heart while you are here," Duncan said as they circled the drive at a sedate pace before taking the animals back to the awaiting stable hands. "You may succumb to the allure of the country yet."

BENEDICT AND DUNCAN joined the family for breakfast. Mrs. Lockhart was dressed and dining with the group, which pleased Benedict. Their stay here had been agreeable to her. She had more color in her cheeks, and more of an appetite.

"What are your plans for the rest of the day," Mrs. Colbourne asked.

Mrs. Lockhart indicated she would spend some time seated outside in the fresh air, while Mr. Colbourne and Duncan were heading to the village on business.

"Mr. Lockhart, I am going for a walk this fine morning, and you must feel free to join us," Alice said.

"Us?"

"Yes, Miss Cecilia is coming and we are going to look for birds."

As if he wanted to look for birds. Benedict wracked his brain for something appropriate to do instead to pass the time. "I think I shall accompany Mother," he said.

"Nonsense," Mrs. Lockhart said. "I shan't be outside long, and it would be a shame for you to miss an opportunity to visit with other young people. You must go with Alice and Miss Cecilia."

Benedict grumbled in protest but did indeed join Alice and Cecilia outside after breakfast. Alice paid him little attention as she and Cecilia made their way toward the trees.

She pointed out a European robin to Cecilia as it perched in a fruit tree at the edge of the garden.

Cecilia paused to watch the little gray bird with the reddish head and throat. It flitted from branch to branch.

"Have you heard the nightingales yet?" Alice asked.

"No, I haven't," Cecilia said.

"Because they are more active in May, you may not hear them as easily this time of year. But if you are out in the evening, they might sing for you."

Cecilia's face lit up, and Benedict couldn't help but notice how different she seemed out here, rather than tucked in a corner during a social engagement. She was confident, not quiet. He wondered if the difference was the location or the company.

"Have you heard nightingales, Mr. Lockhart?" Cecilia asked.

"Several times," he said. "I've heard them here and at my home, Oakwood Manor."

"I've never heard them in London," Cecilia said.

He drew alongside her, noticing how her height made it comfortable for them to walk side-by-side. He didn't have to lean over to converse with her.

"You seem familiar to me, Miss Cecilia. Did you have a season in London?"

She tensed. "Yes, I did. I was not presented at court, but I participated in the social whirl before Papa died. Last season we were in mourning."

"If I did see you, it has been a while then," he said. Somewhere in the back of his mind, he pictured her dancing in a pale green gown, seeing eye to eye with her partner. He couldn't place the location, couldn't put a finger on when he had seen her, but he was almost certain that he had.

"And will you be able to return to London next season?"

Cecilia stopped and stared at him, making him realize his

blunder. "Of course not," she said. "I live here now, in the cottage. My family does not have the means to return, nor do we have family in town to visit."

"Look." Alice pointed up into the branches of a tree. "Do you see it? The tawny owl?"

"I can't see it," Cecilia said, crouching and craning her head. "Oh! There it is."

Benedict had to admit he was impressed by the bird. He'd never paid attention to the local flora and fauna, and it was remarkable to see an owl in the daytime. Cecilia's fascination with it almost made up for his question about returning to London. He hoped she would forgive him once again. First the mud, and now this. He was not usually awkward around a young woman, but he had managed to annoy her twice now. Of course, that would help him win his wager.

When they returned to the house, Alice loaned Cecilia a birding field guide from the Colbourne library before Cecilia headed back to the cottage. Benedict fought the urge to walk her home. He did not want Alice to think he had an interest in Cecilia. Nor did he want Cecilia to think so. Because he was not interested in her. She was everything he did not want. What he needed in a partner was someone who understood the social strata of London, someone who could navigate all obligations of the city, not someone relegated to the countryside. While he and Mother were planning on staying a few more days at Gillingham Park, he found himself wanting to return to Oakwood Manor.

CHAPTER SEVEN

Cecilia's heart pounded as she walked back to the cottage. What if Mr. Lockhart remembered her from London? She had never thought, when they moved to the country, that she would need to worry about people who inhabited both worlds. Though he was unfamiliar to her, it didn't mean they hadn't met before. If Mr. Lockhart remembered her, and the scandal, it would cast a pall over her family, especially if word spread. Would she never be able to leave the past behind her?

"Be a dear," Mama said when she arrived home, "and snip some herbs from the garden. I've ordered a joint of lamb for dinner, and it would be much better with some rosemary."

"Are we expecting company?" Cecilia asked.

Mama sighed and handed her an apron. "No, I am simply tired of economizing. Besides, now that we are more settled, I thought we should celebrate.

Cecilia slipped the apron on and tied it behind her waist. She should have worn a more serviceable dress, but she'd wanted to look decent when she met Alice. Miriam accused her of wanting to impress the gentlemen at Gillingham Park, but she denied it. Although she had to admit Mr. Colbourne and Mr. Lockhart were both attractive and available.

The fragrance of the herbs greeted her as she walked through the garden. One of the things they all missed from London was having a cook. Their maid did her best, but the meals were often bland. Cecilia was more than happy to snip some herbs to liven up the meal. She selected sprigs of rosemary, leaving plenty to grow for the next time, and brought them to the kitchen.

Miriam greeted her as she hung her apron on a hook near the kitchen door. "How were the birds?"

"Fine, thank you. Alice showed me a tawny owl, and I may start taking evening walks to hear a nightingale," Cecilia said. She did not mention Mr. Lockhart.

Miriam's arms were behind her back, and she was unsuccessfully trying to stifle a grin. "You'll never guess what, Sissy."

"I suppose I will not."

"Oh, please try," Miriam said, her eyes sparkling.

"The Queen herself wishes you to come to dinner."

Miriam frowned, jutting out her lower lip in a pout. "Do be serious. Guess again."

"We've a long-lost relative who has invited us to take the waters in Bath."

"If everything you guess is more spectacular than the actual thing, you're bound to be disappointed," Miriam complained, folding her arms in front of her.

"Ahh, you wish me to guess something less grand. All right. We've been invited to tea."

Miriam's jaw dropped. "How did you know? You've spoiled the surprise!"

"I didn't know, I guessed," Cecilia said. "You love to be invited places and I thought an invitation might make you so excited. And you yourself told me it wasn't something grand. Being invited to tea is more commonplace. It seemed a logical guess. But I have no idea who the invitation is from. Surprise me with that."

Miriam smiled. "All right. It is at the Fielding's home, and they have two daughters our age. Won't that be grand to make new friends?"

"Grand," Cecilia said, with more conviction than she felt.

She'd anticipated that after the move, she would have a quiet life here, but it was turning out to be anything but quiet.

"And when are we going to tea?" Cecilia asked.

"Saturday. Mama says we may go to the village for ribbons. I do need to refurbish my old hat. You'll help me, won't you?"

"Yes, and I hope this time the weather is fair and the road is dry," Cecilia said. "We'll make it the most beautiful hat anyone has ever seen."

MIRIAM HAD the chance to show off her hat on Saturday as she and Cecilia walked to the Fielding's home. The weather was warm. Mama had not come with them. She was taken with one of her spells. Melancholy, Cecilia called it. Mama had been good about venturing out into company since the move, but today, she needed to lie down this afternoon rather than go to tea. Cecilia missed Papa, too. She could imagine how Mama felt.

Cecilia gripped Miriam's hand as they entered the Fielding property. "Do you suppose Alice will be here?"

"I don't know," Miriam said. "It would be nice if she were."

But when they arrived at the big house, it became apparent that only the Barnets were invited.

"Wherever is Mrs. Barnet?" Mrs. Fielding asked.

Miriam made apologies for Mrs. Barnet's health.

"Oh dear, I hope she recovers quickly. I hear she is still in mourning. May I ask for how much longer?"

Word was spreading through the community, Cecilia thought in dismay. Because Mama wore mourning clothes while she and Miriam did not, the implication was that she and Miriam were not being respectful of their late father.

"We are past the mourning period these last three months," she said.

If she were surprised by this information, Mrs. Fielding hid it well. She introduced the Barnet sisters to her daughters and escorted them all into the parlor. The Fieldings, it seemed, were quite fond of gardening and had named their daughters Daisy and Rose. Rose was the eldest at age twenty-one, while Daisy was nineteen. They looked enough alike to be twins, and Cecilia sought a way to keep them straight. Both of them had pale complexions and straw-colored hair. Rose's dress had pale pink flowers on it, while Daisy's dress was plain.

"What is it like to live in London?" Daisy asked as Mrs. Fielding poured tea.

"There is always something to do," Miriam replied. "It is rare to have a quiet afternoon alone."

Daisy leaned forward in her chair. "Tell me everything."

London is painful, Cecilia thought. Unforgiving. Eager to pounce on anyone who made a mistake in order to stoke the insatiable gossip machine. But she mustn't say all that, mustn't disappoint their young hostess.

"It's crowded," Cecilia said. "Cabs and carriages, people walking and people on horseback—the streets are busy. The air is dingy in the winter months with all the smoke from heating the houses. And there are rather pungent smells in London that you don't have here."

"Pleasant or unpleasant?" Daisy asked.

"The smells? Mostly unpleasant," Cecilia said, frowning at the memory.

"What Cecilia said is true." Miriam smiled at Daisy. "But London has many shops for hats, gloves, dresses, anything you can imagine. We used to go to a dressmaker. The balls are large and elegant. We ate out or went visiting every week. During the summer months, we met our friends or young gentlemen in Hyde Park. I hope you get to experience it someday."

Daisy's eyes were bright, and Cecilia noticed a tinge of pink on her pale cheeks. She remembered being excited to join Miriam in society. The idea of it held so many possibilities. And yet, the reality was very different. What if she hadn't lived in London where every move was scrutinized? What if she had grown up in the cottage at Gillingham Park with Alice for a friend? Maybe then life would have turned out more like she hoped.

"What do you think of the Colbournes?" Rose asked.

"They have been very gracious," Cecilia replied. This topic was much easier to address. "Alice in particular has made us feel welcome."

"Mr. Duncan Colbourne is quite popular here. Have you spent much time with him?" Daisy asked.

It was inevitable, Cecilia thought, that when young ladies were assembled together the conversation would turn to eligible young men. She had no idea how much time had passed, but she wondered how long they were obligated to stay. Mother's illness might provide the perfect excuse to leave a bit early.

"We've made his acquaintance a few times," Miriam said. "And the acquaintance of his friend, Mr. Lockhart."

Rose nearly swooned. "I have seen Mr. Lockhart in the village. He looks like a fine gentleman. I've heard he has eight thousand pounds a year."

"I suppose that sum would make him attractive no matter what he looked like," Cecilia said.

"I never meant to imply that his money was the only reason to be interested in him. I am sure he is quite fascinating on closer acquaintance."

"I hope you get the opportunity to get to know him better," Miriam said. Cecilia did not share her generosity.

"He is very fond of London," Cecilia said. "I should think he has his eye on a lady there." She had no idea if that were true or not, but it seemed possible.

Rose set down her teacup and crumpled back in her seat. Daisy reached over and squeezed her sister's hand.

"He has not yet met you, Rose. Perhaps you will turn his eye."

A man entered the room and presented an envelope to Mrs. Fielding. She opened it and then passed the note to Rose who managed to read it before Daisy snatched it from her hand.

"A ball! This is the best news. Whatever shall I wear?" She turned to Cecilia. "What will you be wearing?"

"I don't even know if I am invited yet," Cecilia said. She hoped that they were invited, as it would give Miriam a chance to meet more people. Cecilia didn't want to say that she would likely wear a gown from her first season. Something pale and unassuming, something that would allow her to shrink into the background. A dress that would not catch Mr. Lockhart's eye.

CHAPTER EIGHT

enedict was restless and sleep failed to come. He got up and paced the bedroom. Gillingham Park was quiet as the moonlight poured through his window. He peered outside into the night. The cluster of trees at the edge of the property stood inky black against the horizon, backlit by the bright moon.

He could slip outside and take a walk. The day had been unseasonably warm, and it would be a chance to take in the cool air. He was no stranger to the back hallways and servant entrances to the manor. He had explored every nook and cranny with Duncan when they were boys.

Benedict grabbed trousers and tucked in his nightshirt. His shoes felt odd under his bare feet, but he didn't want to take time to find stockings. No servants were up this time of night. In a few hours, the kitchen staff would be hard at work, but for now, everyone was at rest.

Everyone except him. He made his way out of the house and headed for the trees. The owl he'd seen with Alice and Miss Cecilia might be on the prowl tonight. His path was lit by the moon. As he stepped into the darkness of the grove, a sense of calm settled over him. It was a peace he didn't find in the city.

He stood still and let the night wrap around him like a blanket. Insects buzzed and a breeze rustled the leaves. His ears strained to register the unfamiliar noises. Then he heard it. The nightingale.

He wished Miss Cecilia could hear it, too. The thought surprised him. In fact, he was quite surprised that Cecilia was on his mind not only right now, but with great frequency.

A branch snapped. It sounded loud in the night air. Something—or someone—was approaching. The Colbourne's park did not have any deer or many game birds and he doubted a poacher was on the prowl.

"Who's there?" he asked. Whoever it was, he did not wish for them to come upon him unaware.

"Oh."

A female voice.

"Show yourself," Benedict said, wondering who was out at this time in the evening.

"Who are you?" the woman asked, and he heard a tremor in her voice.

"Benedict Lockhart."

Hesitantly, the young lady stepped out from behind a tree, appearing like a wraith in the forest. She was dressed in a simple shift and looked sheepish to have been discovered.

"Mr. Lockhart, whatever are you doing out here?" Cecilia Barnet stepped closer to him in the shadows.

"I could ask you the same thing," he said. His heart beat faster at her proximity. "I could not sleep, so I came to look for the owl."

She laughed. "You are looking for a bird? You did not seem enamored with the activity when we were walking with Alice. But I confess I came here for a bird also. I want to hear a nightingale."

It did not surprise him that she was out here listening for a bird. And yet, he could not picture any of the women he knew in London doing such a thing.

"You are in luck, then. I have heard one sing tonight." He

stepped closer to her, peering at her face in the moonlight. Lilting notes floated through the air.

She gasped and gripped his arm. "Was that it? The nightingale?"

"Yes," he said, happy that he could witness her hearing it for the first time.

"It's beautiful." She tilted her head toward the sound and a ray of moonlight rested on her face.

She was beautiful. The thought flashed through his mind, surprising him. It must be an effect of the moonlight and the lateness of the hour. He was hardly aware of the bird, all of his attention focused on her hand, warming his skin through the thin fabric of his sleeve. He resisted the urge to cover her hand with his.

Several minutes passed as they listened for the bird again, but it remained silent. Benedict didn't speak, not wanting to break the spell. Cecilia pulled her hand away from his arm with a start and glanced down at her feet. Her shoes were old, and Benedict thought he saw a pale patch of skin showing through a hole in the worn leather. Her hair was in a braid that hung well past her shoulders. She reached up to tuck a stray strand behind her ear and took a step away from him.

"I must be going," she said, her voice quiet.

"Stay for a moment and see if we can find the owl," he said.

She hesitated, as if the proposal tempted her. But then she said decisively, "No, Mr. Lockhart. It is inappropriate for me to be here with you."

"Everyone is asleep," he said. "No one will know."

She shook her head, taking another step away from him. "If anyone finds us here—my family won't be able to survive another scandal. Please don't tell anyone that you saw me."

With that, she turned and ran. He took a few steps after her, then stopped and watched her go. She was light on her feet. He shook his head. Miss Cecilia was unexpected. He never knew what she might say or do.

As he walked back to the house, he pondered her words. Another scandal. What was she referring to? It couldn't have happened here where no one seemed to know her. She must be referring to an incident in London. He struggled to recall any such incidents as he paid little attention to gossip. Whatever had happened, she seemed eager to put it behind her. The Barnets were all sufficiently well-mannered that he could not imagine what any of them could have done that was considered scandalous. When he was back in London and this summer was behind him, he might make discreet inquiries. But for now, he would leave it alone.

BENEDICT ROSE EARLY, not tired even after his middle-of-the-night adventure. Miss Cecilia was still on his mind. He kept picturing her face in the shadows, kept remembering the warmth of her hand on his arm. The sooner he returned to Oakwood Manor where he would not encounter her, day or night, the better off he would be. He hoped his mother was feeling well enough to get an early start on their short journey home.

Mrs. Lockhart was already seated at breakfast when he entered the room. She was fully dressed, and her cheeks had lost their pallor.

"Are you feeling better today?" he asked.

"Much better, thank you. I believe spending time at Gillingham Park has been good for both of us. You look healthy and happy, even if you are in the countryside."

He grinned and filled his plate. If she was well enough to tease him, her health was improving. After the meal, he hurried to make sure his belongings were readied for the journey back to Oakwood Manor. He bid farewell to Duncan, Alice, and Mr. and Mrs. Colbourne before helping his mother inside the carriage. Although he much preferred traveling by horseback to the jolting carriage ride, he did not mind spending the time with her.

The road wound past the cottage at the corner of Gillingham Park, and Benedict found, much to his chagrin, that he was staring at the place. He wondered if Miss Cecilia had gotten any sleep last night after their encounter. A flash of blue behind the house caught his eye. It was a woman, barefoot and dark hair tumbling unbound around her shoulders. She went to the garden and bent to pick something. She took no notice of the carriage. Once she had what she wanted from the garden, she ran back to the house with joyful abandon. He couldn't picture any of the London ladies presented to him in the past few months doing that. It seemed so…wild. And inappropriate. So Cecilia.

He frowned and turned away. Last night in the forest already seemed like a dream. Like he had been a visitor to an enchanted world occupied only by the two of them.

"You are lost in thought," Mother said.

"I didn't sleep well last night. I am rather tired," he said.

"I am sorry to hear that. Tonight, you shall sleep in your own bed. Did you enjoy your time with the Colbournes?"

"I did. And you?"

Mother smiled. "Mrs. Colbourne is one of my favorite people. You know that. What did you think of the new tenants?"

"They were agreeable enough," he said, giving her an affectionate grin. He had good relationships with both of his parents, but he relished these easy days with his mother when his father had obligations elsewhere. With his father, the conversations were about running the manor and the London house, staffing, and other business. With his mother, he could discuss most topics. "It is unfortunate they have come to Gillingham Park under less than desirable circumstances."

"That poor family," Mrs. Lockhart said. "It is regrettable that the inheritance did not pass to Mrs. Barnet and her daughters. Society falls short in that regard. In light of their circumstance, however, I am heartened to know you are not smitten with either of them. I presume you will not encourage them?"

"I will not," he promised. He didn't intend to encourage anyone until he returned to London.

"Although," she said, "I do think we'll be obligated to invite them to the ball we are hosting on your behalf. I do owe that to the Colbournes."

The masquerade ball. He had hoped that she had forgotten since she hadn't mentioned it once during their week away.

"We don't have to have a ball, Mother. Maybe it would be best if we didn't. You are feeling better, and we could return to London sooner than expected."

Mrs. Lockhart tsk-tsked at him. "Your father and I wish for you to establish yourself here, at Oakwood Manor. We'd like to see you connected in the community, and in order to accomplish that, we need to provide certain social opportunities for you. We hope to set a high standard for entertainment here. If Oakwood Manor hosts a successful event, others will return the favor. And who knows, you may find a lady here to your liking."

How could he explain to her why the ladies here were not to his taste? This was the world his mother grew up in, and to tell her that he found the women here unrefined would be an offense to her and her family. He would never hurt her that way.

"I'm sure you will create a wonderful event, Mother," Benedict said, resigned. A masquerade ball did not excite him. But he would humor his mother, as he had done many times in the past.

CHAPTER NINE

Cecilia stifled a yawn and tried to focus on her needlework. She had spent time in the garden this morning, and now sat with Mama and Miriam in the parlor. She closed her eyes, thinking of nightingales and Mr. Lockhart in the moonlight. Had she really grabbed his arm? She wondered if he would mention it the next time she saw him and hoped with all her being that he would not.

"Sissy, look!" Miriam roused her and drew her attention to an invitation. "The Sinclairs have invited us to the ball! Come upstairs and help me decide what to wear."

Miriam darted to her room and Cecilia followed at a slower pace. By the time she entered the room, Miriam had already heaped several dresses on the bed. She held up one. "What do you think?"

Cecilia turned a critical eye on the dress. "I think it is torn," she said, pointing out a rip in the skirt. Miriam discarded it and picked up another.

"What about this one?" Miriam held the pale blue gown to her shoulders.

"I think it sets off your hair and your complexion. You should wear it," Cecilia said.

Miriam's gloves, however, were another story. They were graying and one had a very obvious stain. When they showed Mrs. Barnet, she counted out coins and sent them to the village in search of a new pair.

Miriam urged Cecilia to walk at a faster pace. "Whatever is wrong with you today?"

"Nothing," Cecilia said. "I'm a bit tired. That's all." She focused on keeping up with Miriam and they reached the shop in no time. When they went inside, they spotted the Fielding sisters examining a spool of ribbon.

"How lovely to see you!" one of them said.

Cecilia thought it was Daisy, although she wasn't positive it wasn't Rose.

"Did you receive your invitation to the ball?" the other asked.

"Yes," Miriam replied, looking at a pair of white gloves.

"I have it on good authority that both the Colbourne and Lockhart families will be in attendance. I, for one, intend to dance with both Mr. Colbourne and Mr. Lockhart. I will need an introduction to Mr. Lockhart. You have already met him, haven't you? Might I rely on one of the Barnets to make the introduction?"

It would do no harm to introduce the Fielding sisters to Mr. Lockhart, Cecilia mused. They were nice enough, but she doubted they would capture his interest.

"Yes, we'd be happy to," Miriam said.

"What about these, Rose?" Daisy asked, holding up a pair of long gloves in a shimmery fabric. She pulled them on and handed another pair to her sister. They lined up across from each other and began a series of dance steps with Daisy playing the role of the gentleman. Cecilia made a mental note that Daisy had a brown ribbon in her hair today.

"We shall have such fun," Rose declared. "Daisy and I will point out the few men in the neighborhood that you might wish to avoid. We shall claim the hearts of Mr. Lockhart and Mr. Colbourne, and we'll see that you two find suitable men to dance with."

Cecilia resented the implication that the Fielding sisters would claim the two most eligible men in the neighborhood, but she worked to keep her facial expression neutral as

Miriam selected a plain pair of gloves made from good-quality fabric. Cecilia wished she could afford a fancier pair, but she had to admit these gloves would last for quite some time.

After making the purchase, the Barnets bid farewell to the Fielding ladies and hurried home. Miriam kept up a steady stream of conversation as they walked back to Gillingham Park.

"This ball cannot come soon enough," Miriam said. "I did not realize how much I was looking forward to it until this moment. It is as if coming here is bringing us back to life."

"I wish Mama felt that way," Cecilia said. She would have her work cut out for her to get Mama to wear something other than gray.

"Do you think the Fieldings will catch the eye of either Mr. Colbourne or Mr. Lockhart?" Miriam sounded a bit worried.

"We'll make sure they do not. Besides, if they were going to claim Mr. Colbourne's attention, I should think they would have it already. You will shine at this ball, Miriam. I promise."

THE SINCLAIR HOME was larger than the Colbourne's house at Gillingham Park. Cecilia sat up straighter in the carriage. It had been sent for them by the Colbournes, and while she appreciated their generosity, she resented having to accept charity. She missed Papa's carriage and the fine horses that pulled it.

Footmen stood outside waiting to greet the guests and help them from their carriages. Their finery made Cecilia self-conscious about her own attire. The light brown of her dress would not catch anyone's attention tonight. The dress was unadorned but had the redeeming factor of being long enough to cover her worn shoes.

Miriam, too, was impressed by the grandeur of the home. "You should have worn your green dress" she said.

It was true. Her green dress was more flattering. But it reminded her of her worst day of the London season and she was loathe to put it on again.

Cecilia took extra care getting out of the carriage, barely letting her gloved hand touch that of the footman who came to assist them. No awkward stumbles this time.

Once inside, they were greeted by Mr. and Mrs. Sinclair, a stately older couple. It wasn't long before the music started and people paired up to dance. Cecilia used her height advantage to scan the room for people she recognized. It would make the evening far more pleasant if she were able to converse with Alice Colbourne.

She spied Mr. Lockhart deep in conversation with a man she did not know. She turned away from him--reticent to talk to him after their late-night encounter--and bumped into the Fielding sisters.

"We're glad we found you," one of them said. Cecilia really did need to learn how to keep them straight. "Now you may introduce us to Mr. Lockhart!"

"He's so dashing!" the other sister said.

Cecilia sighed. She regretted that Miriam had promised to make introductions. Now, Miriam was nowhere in sight, and she would have to fulfill the obligation. What if Mr. Lockhart brought up seeing her wandering at midnight? And what would he think of her shabby dress and dingy gloves? She wished Mama had let her stay home tonight.

One of the Fieldings gripped her hand. "Please, Miss Cecilia, take me and Rose over to meet him."

Daisy was in a white dress tonight, while Rose wore peach. Cecilia trailed after the sisters, slowing as they approached Mr. Lockhart. Daisy raised her gloved hand to cover her mouth as she giggled in excitement. Mr. Lockhart overheard and raised an eyebrow. He did not seem the type to find giggling women attractive.

When the gentleman to whom he was speaking excused himself, Daisy surged forward. Rose hung back, tilting her chin down and looking up at Mr. Lockhart through her long eyelashes. Cecilia recognized their behavior as flirting, although she'd never successfully engaged in it herself.

Mr. Lockhart's gaze passed over the Fielding sisters and locked on Cecilia's eyes instead. "Miss Cecilia, how good it is to see you," he said.

Cecilia could not ignore the flutter that began in her stomach and spread to her fingers and toes. Was he happy to see her or was he being polite? She wished she could ask Miriam or Alice to decode his meaning. Daisy nudged her arm.

"Mr. Lockhart, may I introduce my friends to you? Miss Rose Fielding and Miss Daisy," she said. There. She'd made proper introductions. Now she could disappear into a corner and wait out the rest of the dance.

The musicians began playing and several couples lined up in formation. The tune was lively and Cecilia couldn't help tapping her foot in rhythm. Mr. Lockhart made small talk with the Fieldings. Daisy fanned her face as if she might swoon.

"He is even more handsome in person! And such a gentleman," she whispered to Cecilia. "I hope he asks me to dance."

Cecilia spotted a vacant chair in the corner and excused herself from the sisters. She had no desire to dance, and she didn't want to engage in conversation with Mr. Lockhart. Seated in the corner, she could enjoy the music. While she hadn't missed much about balls, she had missed the music.

Mr. Lockhart accompanied Rose to the dance floor and

Cecilia watched with interest. While Rose was quite animated and intent on conversation, Mr. Lockhart moved through the dance steps mechanically, barely speaking. Twice he missed steps. Once he even tromped on Rose's foot and she let out a little squeal. Cecilia found it hard to believe he could be such a bad dancer, but maybe he was. Maybe that was one of his flaws.

The dance finished and Mr. Lockhart hurried to the other side of the room, abandoning Rose in the middle of the floor. Cecilia wondered how he could seem appealing in a forest of trees and obnoxious here in a crowd. What was he like in London?

Miriam appeared beside her. "Come, Sissy, you mustn't hide here in the corner. I found Alice and we should allow her to introduce us to people."

Cecilia reluctantly left the chair and followed Miriam. Rose Fielding stopped them. "Did you see Mr. Lockhart dance with me? He is handsome, but what manners! The few times he did speak to me, it was to talk about other ladies in the room. And my poor foot," she said. "He may be the most eligible man here, but there is nothing to recommend him."

"Except eight thousand pounds," Daisy said. "I might have more luck than you did, Rose. If he sees me dancing, I'm sure he'll ask me later."

Cecilia doubted that, but she said nothing. Daisy eyed the crowd for likely dance partners and, spotting a pair of gentlemen they knew, left the Barnets. Cecilia watched the way Daisy and Rose made eye contact with the men. Rose touched her hair, while Daisy fingered her necklace. They both had radiant smiles and leaned toward the gentleman who was speaking to them. No matter how she tried, Cecilia could not interact that way with men and make it appear natural.

"Would you care to dance, Miss Cecilia?"

Cecilia jumped, startled. Duncan Colbourne bowed beside her. Cecilia longed to say yes, but Miriam should be the one dancing. Scandal-free, appropriate Miriam had more of a chance of making a good match, and Cecilia would not get in the way of that.

"Thank you ever so much, Mr. Colbourne, but I'm feeling rather faint," Cecilia said. "I'm afraid I must decline your generous offer and find a chair. Perhaps you would dance with Miriam instead?"

"I am sorry you are unwell," he said with a frown. "May I get you anything?"

Cecilia shook her head. "I see a chair by my mother, and I shall make my way toward it and watch the dance."

"I will save a dance for you later," Duncan said. He offered his arm to Miriam. "Would you care to dance, Miss Barnet?"

Miriam winked at Cecilia. "Why thank you, Mr. Colbourne." They joined the couples on the floor and Cecilia sat on the chair in the corner. She could not see Mr. Lockhart anywhere. The Fielding sisters, however, had secured partners and were joining the dance.

"You should not have introduced the Fieldings to Mr. Lockhart," Mrs. Barnet said when Cecilia took the chair beside her.

It would be nice if Mama acknowledged her skill in getting Mr. Colbourne to dance with Miriam. She could have been on the dance floor instead.

"Someone else would have made the introduction if I had not, Mama. I was being polite."

Mama frowned, and Cecilia focused on the dancers. Miriam's eyes sparkled and her smile was radiant. Mr. Colbourne was light on his feet. Miriam's gloved hand met Mr. Colbourne's as they executed the dance steps, and it was evident from their smiles, from the way Mr. Colbourne dipped his head to listen to her, that they were enjoying their conversation. How different it was from the way Mr. Lockhart danced with Miss Fielding.

Cecilia leaned back in her chair, her foot still tapping in time to the music. When the dance finished, Miriam came to find her.

"It's hot, Cecilia. Come, let's go outside." Miriam led her across the large room to the double doors which opened to a balcony. The night air was cool on Cecilia's face. She crossed the balcony and rested her arms on the rail.

Voices from the garden caught their attention. A man and a woman walked toward them, pausing near a bench set to the side of the manicured path. Cecilia leaned forward, trying to hear the conversation.

"It is a beautiful evening, Mr. Lockhart," the young lady said, gazing up at the man beside her.

"Thank you for showing me the garden," he replied. "I must, however, return to the ball. I have promised the next two dances. You must understand that my time is in high demand."

It was callous of him, Cecilia thought, but perhaps not unexpected. She pitied the girl. Other couples were wandering the garden paths. Nothing here would harm the young lady's reputation. But Mr. Lockhart's comments stung. He did not offer his arm as he turned and walked back to the building. The young woman followed him, her posture like a wilted flower. This version of Mr. Lockhart was a man who would be careless about who his carriage splashed. It was hard to reconcile what she was witnessing with the man who was listening to nightingales under the moonlight.

"You know I wanted to talk to you about Mr. Colbourne away from Mama, don't you?" Miriam asked, tearing Cecilia's focus away from Mr. Lockhart and the young woman.

I'm glad he danced with you," Cecilia said.

"Mr. Colbourne was such a gentleman," Miriam said. "He was a very adequate partner."

"Only adequate?" Cecilia teased.

Miriam sighed. "He is more than adequate, and I do like him, but Sissy, I doubt my appeal to him. What do I have that would make a man of his standing desire a partnership with me?"

Cecilia's heart sank. The injustice of it all filled her with anguish. Miriam was worthy of any man here, yet without their father and his economic standing, it was possible that she would be relegated to a less-than-desirable match. It pained her to picture Miriam married to an old widower with grown children. No, Miriam deserved better.

"Give it time, Miriam. We've not lived here very long. Once people get to know you, once they see your goodness, you will find a suitor. You'll see. But now you should return to the ball and enjoy the evening."

"Only if you come with me," Miriam said. Cecilia would much rather stroll through the garden, but she did not dare go alone. Reluctantly, she followed Miriam only to be accosted by Mr. Lockhart.

"I've come for our promised dances," he said.

Cecilia stared at him. Was that a twinkle in his eye? Did he find this amusing?

"I am not senile," she replied. "I believe I would know if I had promised a dance to you, not to mention two dances."

CHAPTER TEN

enedict stepped closer and spoke quietly. "Miss Cecilia, I request the pleasure of your company for the next two dances. I must escape Miss Evans."

He was aware that the woman in question lingered nearby. His eyes found Cecilia's and held their gaze. "Please."

He ignored Miss Evans and offered his arm to Cecilia. She glanced about. People were watching, and he hoped that would not make her uncomfortable.

"Of course you may reject my offer," he said, leaning his head toward her so that no one else would hear. "But if you do choose to dance with me now, it may secure your standing in the neighborhood and make things easier for you and your sister. Whether deserved or not, the name Lockhart does have a great deal of prestige here."

Cecilia's jaw was set in a most-determined look. She took his arm. "I would be delighted to dance with you, but I would prefer it if you danced with Miriam. If you do that, I shall not mention the mud again, and we will consider things between us to be resolved."

Benedict flinched as she mentioned the mud. He did rather regret making such a bad first impression on her. Cecilia Barnet was growing on him. Perhaps they would end up with a friendship like the one he had with Alice Colbourne.

He smiled at her. "You drive a hard bargain, Miss Cecilia, but I would be happy to dance with Miss Barnet. After this set."

During the first dance, Benedict found that he could not keep his eyes off Cecilia, much to his chagrin. She was slightly disheveled, her complexion a bit rosy. Her jaw was tense, as if she would not give him the satisfaction of enjoying the dance. It was his habit to move through the steps without speaking, but tonight he wanted to draw her out in conversation.

"Are you settled? In the cottage, I mean?" he asked.

Her expression was unreadable. "Do you truly wish to know if we have unpacked the bedding and if we are getting by with our limited staff? What are you asking, Mr. Lockhart?"

Her bluntness caught him by surprise. "I mean you no harm, Miss Cecilia. I know it is an adjustment for me each time I come to the country, and I cannot imagine what it is like for you and your family after the loss of your father. I apologize if I've upset you."

"Upsetting people is what you appear to be good at," Cecilia said.

He paused, disrupting the rhythm of the steps. Was she angry with him? Or was she laughing at him?

"I'm afraid I get rather too much practice," he said, smiling at her. "Perhaps you could correct me on my behavior from time to time."

He was rewarded with a smile that lit up her entire face. When she smiled, she no longer looked like a gawky young lady on the brink of womanhood but rather a young woman who was sure of herself. More confident. He had to admit that he found it rather appealing.

As the dance drew to a close, he scrambled for something more to say to her, something to keep the conversation going. "Have you enjoyed any more walks by moonlight?"

Her eyes darted to the other dancers, as if she wished to

make sure no one could overhear. "You promised not to say anything," she said.

"I assure you I have told no one," Benedict replied.

"If you must know, I have not had any more midnight excursions. Now that I have heard the nightingales, I prefer to sleep."

They faced each other, waiting for the second dance to begin. Several couples left the dance floor while new partnerships joined the line. As the music began, Benedict and Cecilia separated and circled with other partners before coming back together. Cecilia had an impish expression on her face.

"When you danced with Miss Fielding, you appeared to suffer from a bout of clumsiness. Have you recovered?"

Benedict fought to keep from smiling, but failed, revealing his dimple to her. "You have found me out, Miss Cecilia. You see through me."

"Why pretend to be clumsy?" she asked.

"Did Miss Fielding recommend me to you after our dance?"

"She did not," Cecilia said.

"Then my ruse worked," he replied.

Cecilia wrinkled her forehead. "You were impolite to her intentionally?"

"It's my way of discouraging unwanted attention."

"What are you hiding from, Mr. Lockhart? Are you afraid of people seeing the real you?"

He missed a dance step but recovered quickly. "I assure you that I have nothing to hide," he said as the music ended. He held her gaze, and for a moment, he wished he were alone with her again in the forest.

Cecilia curtsied and thanked him for the dance. "Remember my sister," she said, and scurried away.

Benedict sighed. He made his way through the line of

ladies surrounding the dance floor and found Miss Barnet in conversation with Duncan and Miss Colbourne. She was, at first glance, more refined than her younger sister. More polished. He wondered why she hadn't been selected already as someone's wife. He knew she did not possess a fortune, but there were plenty of available men for whom that was not an issue. Was it her father's death that prevented her from making a good match?

She graciously accepted his invitation to dance. Once on the dance floor, he kept his manners impeccable, making sure Miss Barnet was seen in the best possible way. She was an appealing partner, and he was certain she could attract an eligible match.

"You had much to say to my sister," Miriam observed.

"She had much to say for herself," he offered. "Tell me, have I met you both before? In London?"

"Last season we were in mourning. I am certain we haven't met."

He shook his head. "Perhaps the season before. You seem rather familiar, as does your sister."

"I don't remember you," she said. "I've heard the Lockhart name, but I don't remember being introduced. Perhaps you are thinking of someone else." Her face was closed off, and she didn't make eye contact with him. He had the nagging feeling that he had met her before, that he did know the Barnet sisters, but he couldn't place how he had known them. Maybe she was right. Maybe he was mistaken.

"Have you siblings, Mr. Lockhart?" She seemed eager to change the subject.

"I have a married sister and a younger brother who is in school," he said.

They continued to make small talk until the end of the dance. Benedict escorted Miss Barnet back to her sister and went to find Duncan. Plenty of ladies hoped for a turn around the ballroom with him, but he had no interest in spending much more time dancing. The Barnet sisters already had reason not to like him, and if he were to win this wager with Duncan, he could use that to his advantage. Paying them attention, dancing with them when he knew they had no interest in him, would make the other young ladies annoyed with him, and that was exactly what he wanted.

"Both Barnet sisters?" Duncan asked. "Impressive. Have they forgiven you for the mud bath?"

"Yes, I believe so. I may not be in their good graces, but I think they find me tolerable now."

Duncan chuckled. "I'm glad you've made peace with them. That will make our future encounters easier. How is your mother today?"

Benedict fiddled with his cravat. "She is a bit improved. I believe the country air suits her. However, she did not feel up to joining me tonight. I hope she is better by the Harrison's garden party."

"Will you be attending?" Duncan asked.

"Yes, if Mother is up to it."

"You are a devoted son. I'll see you later, friend."

"Wait, where are you going?" Benedict asked, dreading being left alone with potential dance partners circling.

"I need to introduce my tenants to the Harrisons. Perhaps they will enjoy getting to know people at a garden party."

Benedict pulled a face. That was all he needed…the Barnets to be everywhere he went. Still, if that was the best plan Duncan had to make him lose the wager, he was very secure in his potential to win. Miss Barnet was in his estimation, forgettable. And Miss Cecilia…Miss Cecilia could be an interesting ally.

As he worked his way through the crowd of people seeking refreshment, he came up behind the Fielding sisters. Benedict paused, not wishing to draw their attention.

Daisy Fielding noticed him and rushed toward him, smiling. Miss Fielding was quick to follow.

"We saw you dancing with Miss Cecilia," Daisy said. "I was surprised you would want to be seen with her considering the way she was dressed."

"I saw nothing wrong with her dress. It was appropriate for the occasion," Benedict said.

"Her gloves were dirty. How could you bear to touch them?" Rose asked.

Benedict had no recall of the condition of Cecilia's gloves. He'd been too captivated by her.

Rose chimed in. "She needs a dressmaker. It's embarrassing that the Barnets are here. It would seem Mr. Colbourne has taken pity on them, securing them an invitation. Like poor relations."

Daisy was quick to join in, as if she had to better her sister. "I heard that one of them was embroiled in a scandal in London and that they had to leave in shame."

Benedict was about to answer when he saw Cecilia and Miriam standing nearby. How much had they heard? Miriam's face flushed with anger while Cecilia turned pale. Her lip trembled. Before he could react, Miriam put her arm around Cecilia's waist and steered her through the crowd. The Fielding sisters were still talking, and he interrupted them.

"I can assure you Miss Fielding, Miss Daisy, that Mr. Colbourne did not invite the Barnets here out of pity. They have every right to be here as they are guests of the Sinclairs. The only scandal I am aware of is two ladies speaking unkindly about people they pretended to befriend. And it would benefit you both to remember that." He walked away before they could respond.

CHAPTER
ELEVEN

"I'm not going," Cecilia said. The thought of attending the garden party or any other social event filled her with dread. Not only had Rose and Daisy been cruel in their comments about her, but they had also made those comments to Mr. Lockhart. How could she possibly face any of them again? The thought of a governess position far from here was more attractive than ever. How she longed to be somewhere where no one knew her.

"I insist that you go. Get dressed. The Colbournes are sending a carriage," Mama said.

Of course they were. Cecilia had appreciated their kindness at first, but now she chafed under the necessity of relying on others. If they did not have their own transportation, they were not able to leave when they wanted.

Miriam came to help her with her hair. "Don't fret, Cecilia. We shall go and hold our heads high. The opinion of the Fielding sisters should not matter to either one of us. The Colbournes have more standing here, and they have been most kind."

"I shall go," Cecilia said, "but please don't leave me alone with anyone."

Miriam gave her a hug. "I will not. I promise."

As THE GUESTS gathered in the grove for the luncheon, Cecilia escaped with Alice and Miriam to walk around the

Harrison's property. They made their way to the lake, leaving the picnickers milling around under leafy trees while the food was being set out. A small gray bird with a reddish-orange face and throat hopped near a hedge.

"European robin," Cecilia said. Alice gave her arm a squeeze.

"You are a quick study. We'll have you knowing all the local birds in no time."

They reached the edge of the pond. "This is a beautiful place," Cecilia said. It was peaceful as the water rippled gently in the breeze. A few stray clouds reflected white on the water.

"It is a lovely place," Alice agreed. "Too bad the Harrisons don't have any more eligible sons. They married off the last one this past winter."

"All the more reason to enjoy this gathering," Miriam said. "No social pressure."

"Ah, but these gatherings can have the most social pressure. Other mothers will be sizing up both of you as either prospects for their sons or as competition for their daughters."

Cecilia sighed. It would be much nicer to enjoy the scenery without having to play these games. "Speaking of eligible sons, I noticed that Duncan danced with Miriam more than once at the Sinclair's ball. Has he any interest in her?"

Alice tipped her face toward the sky and laughed. "Duncan is spoken for, I'm afraid. It's best if you put your focus elsewhere."

Disappointment flashed across Miriam's face, but she recovered quickly. "We shall be on our best behavior today so that we do not scare off any other prospects."

Cecilia squeezed Miriam's hand. "Perhaps we have nothing to worry about. The way the Fielding sisters are talking about us will eliminate us from any competition," she said.

"What are you talking about?" Alice asked.

Miriam filled her in about the sisters demeaning them to Mr. Lockhart.

"I'd love to give them a piece of my mind," Alice said. "If they were here, I would."

"No, please don't," Cecilia said. "It will only make things worse."

Alice fumed for several more minutes. Cecilia took comfort in the idea that the Colbournes truly might be their friends.

Miriam gestured toward the picnic area. "The food appears to be ready. Come, we'll have more time to wander later."

Reluctantly, Cecilia followed Alice and Miriam back up the little grassy hill where a feast awaited them. It was an impressive assortment of sliced beef, roasted fowl, breads, jams, and fresh fruit. Cecilia had little appetite, though, and it was only with Miriam's coaxing that she set some food on her plate. Mama had secured them a spot on the same blanket as Mr. Lockhart and his mother.

Cecilia hung back. "Miriam, I cannot go over there," she whispered.

"We must," Miriam said. "Hold your head high. We've done nothing wrong."

When they approached the blanket, Mr. Lockhart rose to his feet. Cecilia refused to meet his eye. She sat on the corner of the blanket furthest from him.

Mrs. Lockhart's face was rounder and had more color to her cheeks than when Cecilia first met her. She greeted Cecilia with a brilliant smile. "It's nice to see you and Miss Barnet again. Tell me, what do you think of my rogue son?"

"Mother," Mr. Lockhart protested. "Please don't spoil everyone's appetite by talking about me."

Miriam took a delicate bite of food leaving a response to Cecilia.

Cecilia frowned, She hated being put on the spot like this, and she could not look at Mr. Lockhart after her humiliation. Still, Miriam was right. She had done nothing wrong. She cleared her throat and said, "I know that he is not fond of dancing, has no fear of mud puddles, and prefers game birds to songbirds. What else do I need to know about him?"

Mrs. Lockhart leaned toward Cecilia with a conspiratorial tone. "He is not yet convinced of the pleasures of the countryside."

Mrs. Barnet chimed in. "I believe he needs the right companion to help him appreciate it. Perhaps, Cecilia, you might show Mr. Lockhart the virtues of the lake after the meal."

Cecilia choked on a piece of food and coughed. How could Mama make such a suggestion? Cecilia would rather help the servants clean up the mess than walk with Mr. Lockhart to the lake, but she refrained from saying it.

"You and Miss Barnet and Miss Colbourne and Mr. Colbourne should all go," Mrs. Lockhart said. "It would give me a great deal of satisfaction to see all of you young people happily entertained."

"I am sure they would be delighted," Mrs. Barnet said. Before Cecilia could come up with an excuse, it was all arranged.

She lingered over the meal as long as possible, but when Mr. Colbourne came to escort them, she rose to her feet and joined the party. She longed to talk to Alice, but Miriam and Duncan were walking with Alice between them. That left Cecilia with Mr. Lockhart.

He seemed in no hurry and let the others gain a small lead over them. He did not speak, and neither did she. Her embarrassment over the incident at the ball made it a strain to make conversation. Still, it might be better if she spoke first.

"Have you no ladies to offend today?"

He snorted, and then quickly regained his composure. "No new ones, I'm afraid. Are you keeping score?"

"I might be," she said, pulling gently at her bonnet strings. "I know of Miss Evans, my sister, and myself."

"You are behind, I'm afraid. You should add Miss Fielding and Miss Daisy to the list. I was quite offended by them, and I let them know."

Cecilia stopped. "You did?"

"Yes, at the ball. Their behavior was unacceptable. You and Miss Barnet did not deserve that treatment."

She never expected Mr. Lockhart to defend her. He had no reason to that she could imagine.

"Thank you," she said.

"You should know that I think I have put off Miss Martin and her sister, Miss Anne. That is why they are not joining our walk to the lake." He smiled at her.

Cecilia wrinkled her forehead. "But you've only been here for a short while. You are working rather quickly. However did you do that?"

"I won't share my secrets," Mr. Lockhart said. "But know this, I plan to escape all of you ladies this summer."

"You are off to a good start. I won't interfere with your plan. But I hear you are most eligible. Are you waiting for a London lady to steal your heart?"

He turned toward her, a lock of brown hair tumbling over his eye. Cecilia found herself resisting the urge to brush it away.

"Yes, a London lady. And you? Are you looking for a country lord?"

They reached the edge of the lake, but instead of joining the others near the dock, they stopped beside a rock overlooking the water.

"I must assure you that I am seeking no such person," Cecilia said. "I would like a good match for my sister, Miriam. She is deserving, and I fear with our father's passing, she may be overlooked."

She watched Duncan laugh at something Miriam said. Duncan and Miriam seemed comfortable together. She was saddened that he was promised to someone else.

The water on the pond had settled to an almost perfect stillness as the cooling breeze died down. Two elegant white swans glided across the water.

"Did you know, Miss Cecilia, that the king owns all of the swans in England?"

Cecilia wondered at Benedict's change in conversation. Was he mentioning birds to tease her? Despite her limited knowledge of birds, she did indeed know that the swans were possessed by the crown.

"And yet, can one really own a swan?" she asked. "It seems to me these two are free to fly wherever, without asking the king's approval."

"And does that appeal to you? The freedom to move where you would like?"

She turned away from him and watched the swans. "I am a bit envious of their freedom. Society has many constraints and decides who is worthy of love and approval or who shall be shunned. It seems simpler to be a swan."

Mr. Lockhart took a step toward her, his shoulder nearly touching hers. "I've been told that swans stay with the same partner throughout their lives. That is an admirable quality."

The sleeve of his jacket brushed against her shoulder. He paused, letting it linger. Cecilia didn't mind his closeness. He was the perfect height. If he were to give her an embrace, her cheek would nestle on his shoulder. She gazed up into his brown eyes.

"Loyalty is also an admirable quality," she said.

"Loyalty, freedom of choice, freedom to fly. I am envious of the swans indeed," he said.

The moment was frozen in time. Cecilia lost awareness of the group, the water, even the swans. All her attention was on Mr. Lockhart—how his arm touched hers, how their breathing fell into the same rhythm. Longing for companionship filled her heart, and she knew deep inside that while she wished for a partner for Miriam, she could no longer deny that she wanted a relationship for herself.

She pushed the thought aside. Mr. Lockhart had his heart set on a London lady, and Cecilia would never be that again.

Alice's shriek of delight as she skipped a stone on the still water pulled Cecilia out of her reverie. Mr. Lockhart offered her his arm. "May I escort you to the others?"

As they walked away from the swampy edge of the lake, her foot slipped. Mr. Lockhart caught her with an arm around her waist. He lifted her to more stable ground, and as he set her in place, his arm lingered. At first, Cecilia enjoyed the embrace, but then she realized she was in full view of their party. She panicked. Not here. Not again. She was only beginning to settle into this neighborhood and the last thing she needed was a new scandal. Once she was steady on her feet, she pulled away from Mr. Lockhart.

"Are you all right?" he asked. "Your shoe is muddy. Here, let me."

He pulled out a handkerchief and squatted down to clean her shoe but before he touched her, Cecilia turned and ran.

"Cecilia, wait!" Miriam called after her.

"I'll go," Alice said, and followed Cecilia away from the others. She caught up to her and reached for her arm.

"Cecilia dear, what happened? Was Benedict improper? If he was, I shall give him a very stern reprimand."

Bending slightly to catch her breath, Cecilia paused. "No, but I slipped on the wet ground, and he caught me. He kept me from falling. If anyone saw…." Cecilia shook her head in misery. "I can't be caught in a scandal. I'll destroy every chance that Miriam has."

Alice raised her eyebrows at Cecilia. "Scandal? You were not alone with him, and all of us saw that he was only coming to your assistance. Please don't let it worry you. Everyone in our group has the greatest discretion, and we are all quite fond of you. Think nothing of it."

Cecilia wanted to believe Alice but struggled to do so. She knew how an innocent moment could be misinterpreted and spread by gossip. It took so little to ruin so much.

"Please come back with me," Alice said, gesturing toward her brother at the pond. Cecilia saw Mr. Lockhart staring after her. She could not face him now. Not only had he gripped her waist and sent chills all through her, but then she had rebuffed him and run away, making an awkward situation worse. If she could disappear in this moment, she would. Instead, she squared her shoulders and determined that she would rejoin Mama.

"Please tell them I am not feeling well and will be with my mother until it is time to leave."

Alice sighed. "Are you sure? What shall I tell Mr. Lockhart?"

"That I am grateful he saved me from the mud." With that, she headed off to find her mother.

CHAPTER TWELVE

That evening, Benedict paced in his study, mentally rehearsing his conversation with Cecilia. Everything had been going well. In fact, he found himself attracted to her out by the lake. And he thought she'd felt the same until she slipped in the mud. He'd put his arm around her to keep her upright, and then to his surprise, she ran away and avoided him the rest of the afternoon.

He couldn't figure out what he had done wrong. Having seen her reaction to splashing her with mud in his carriage, he knew she did not want him to let her fall in the mud by the lake, but what made her flee? She left the garden party before he had a chance to speak with her, and now, he wondered how he could make amends.

And when. His only hope was that she would attend the masquerade at Oakwood Manor. For the first time, he had a reason to look forward to the event. He had nothing on his calendar where he might see Cecilia before then, and now he must hope that she would come to the ball.

The door to his study swung open and his mother stepped inside. "What is bothering you, son?"

Benedict sighed. He didn't want to discuss Cecilia with his mother. In fact, he didn't want to discuss her with anyone. His ever-growing interest in her was unlike anything else he'd ever experienced, and he was reticent to share his feelings and open himself up to the scrutiny of others. He knew the Barnets were not the sort of family that his parents would want him to select a partner from.

Mother crossed the room and sat in a chair. "Was it something from the party this afternoon?"

"I'm fine, Mother. I am restless here, that is all. How many garden parties and early morning rides can one man take?"

Mrs. Lockhart laughed. "It is not busy in London right now. You will be back in plenty of time for the next season. Perhaps this will brighten your week. Your sister, Kate, will arrive tomorrow with the children. That should keep you occupied as we finish planning the masquerade."

She was right. Kate was always entertaining, as were her two children. Oliver, in particular, was his favorite. The boy was serious and inquisitive. His niece, Margaret, grew in personality every time he saw her. She was a miniature copy of her mother.

"It shall be good to have them here. I haven't seen them for quite a while. Is Father planning to join us?"

Mrs. Lockhart shook her head. "I'm afraid not. Mr. Lockhart and Kate's husband will both remain in London on business. But I have news you will appreciate. I am feeling much better, and after the masquerade, I shall be ready to return to London with you."

To his surprise, Benedict was not overjoyed at the news. Now it was more imperative than ever that he resolve things with Cecilia at the ball. He did not want her to remain on the list of ladies he had offended. Before he returned to London, he needed to find out why she was upset with him.

"I am looking forward to the masquerade, Mother. It shall be a grand event, and then I will happily return to London with you."

Mrs. Lockhart rose from her chair. "Tomorrow will be a busy day, Benedict. Why don't you get some sleep, and I'll see you in the morning."

"I'm glad you are feeling better, Mother. Oakwood Manor has been good to you." He kissed his mother's cheek as she left the room, but it was a while before he was tired enough to retire for the night. Even then, he did not fall asleep easily. It would probably be best if he did not talk to Cecilia at all. If he had made her uncomfortable or upset again, perhaps that was how he should leave it. After all, his return to London was imminent, and then he would not be seeing her again. Maybe it would be less painful to let her go.

But he found himself wanting to leave things with her on good terms. And he wouldn't mind dancing again with her, either.

BENEDICT WAS unprepared for something heavy to land on him the following morning. He sat up, struggling to remove the heavy object, which turned out to have arms, legs, and burbling laughter.

"Uncle Benedict!" the voice said. "Wake up!"

"I'm awake," he said. "Get off me, you rascal!"

He tickled Oliver, who laughed and struggled to get away. "Grandmother says that you are to come to breakfast and then you may take me to the stables."

Benedict ran his hand through his hair, making it stand on end. He had finally slept, images of Cecilia slipping in and out of his dreams. Oliver would be a welcome distraction today.

"Hurry, hurry, hurry!" Oliver chanted as he bounced from the room.

Resisting the urge to fall back on his pillows, pull the covers over his head, and go back to sleep, Benedict swung his legs out of the bed and placed his feet squarely on the floor. He heard voices downstairs. His mother and his sister, he guessed.

He went to the basin and splashed water on his face. His

valet knocked and entered the room, helping him to dress. Benedict hurried downstairs to join his family. Kate greeted him with a hug, and little Margaret hid behind her mother's skirts, sucking on a finger and staring at him with wide blue eyes.

As they settled around the table and filled their plates, Kate studied him. "Not sleeping well, brother?" she asked.

He shook his head. "Not last night, I'm afraid."

Kate grinned at him. "Does she have a name?"

Benedict choked on a mouthful of food. He gripped his napkin and covered his mouth, coughing into it.

"Some young lady seems to have captured your attention enough to disturb your sleep," Kate teased. "Surely she has a name."

He shook his head. "If she exists, I have not met her," he insisted. He was suddenly shy about discussing Cecilia with anyone in the household.

Kate returned to her food and seemed to accept his response, but he caught her looking at him more than once, her lips quirking upward in the hint of a smile. Benedict frowned. How could he possibly sort out what he felt for Cecilia Barnet under the scrutiny of his observant sister? Keeping Oliver occupied seemed like the best recourse.

"After breakfast, I'd like to take Oliver out to see the horses," Benedict said.

"I think that is a splendid idea," Mrs. Lockhart said. "You may keep him occupied while we make plans for the masquerade."

Benedict never thought he would ever want to spend hours in the company of an eight-year-old, but now that was exactly what he planned to do. Miss Cecilia Barnet was changing him in more ways than one.

CHAPTER
THIRTEEN

Miriam met Cecilia upstairs where Cecilia had dresses spread out on Miriam's bed.

"Where were you?" Cecilia said, frowning.

Miriam shrugged. "I went for a walk."

"You have never been much of a walker," Cecilia said. "Were you walking around Gillingham Park?"

"Sissy, I know that Alice said her brother was promised to someone, but I have twice encountered him while out walking and he has never indicated that to me. In fact, I am fond of spending time with him."

"You must not lose your heart to him, Miriam, or it shall be broken. If he hasn't been honest with you about his attachment, then you must be careful. And you must not meet him alone again. You have a reputation to protect."

"Duncan would do nothing to harm me," Miriam said.

"Duncan? Not Mr. Colbourne?" Worry filled Cecilia's mind. What was Miriam up to? This could have no good end.

"He asked me to call him Duncan and I agreed," Miriam said, her cheeks flushing pink.

"I fear this cannot end well," Cecilia said.

"Why not?" Miriam asked. "I am as deserving of his attention as the other young ladies here. Or don't you agree?"

"You know I do, Miriam, but I don't want to see you hurt."

"Duncan is kind and thoughtful. We've known that from the very first time we met him. I still have his handkerchief. You must trust me," Miriam said.

The maid entered the open door of the room. "Miss Alice Colbourne to see you," she said.

Miriam stepped closer to the bed and fingered one of the dresses as Alice entered the room. Cecilia was tempted to ask Alice again about Duncan but knew Miriam would never forgive her if she did.

"Whatever brings you here this morning?" Cecilia asked.

"I came to see how you were faring after the picnic," Alice replied. She looked meaningfully at Cecilia. "Did the mud come out of your shoe?"

Cecilia shook her head. "I'm afraid it is rather stained. I am left with my boots and little else to wear. We are choosing dresses for the masquerade ball, and now that you are here, you may help us."

Alice walked slowly past the clothing spread out on Miriam's bed. Cecilia imagined seeing the items through Alice's eyes. Her own dresses in particular were worn and shabby, and she knew for a fact that at least one of them was too short, having been purchased before her last season. Unlike Miriam, Cecilia had grown at least another inch during their year of mourning. Miriam's dresses were in slightly better condition, but each of them had already been worn at various social events here in town. None of them were fit to draw attention at a masquerade ball.

Alice selected one of the dresses, assessing its size and length. She held it up to Miriam and Cecilia in turn, then laid it back on the bed. "Are these the gowns you must choose from?"

"Yes," Miriam said with a sigh. "Cecilia's dresses are in worse shape than mine."

"A dress for Miriam is the most important," Cecilia said. "I might not even attend the ball, but Miriam should not miss it."

"Some of my dresses from last season never fit properly

or were a color that did not go with my complexion," Alice said. "It would do me a great service if you would take them off my hands. Of course, they may need altering before they are fit for you to wear."

Cecilia bit her lip. Although she appreciated Alice's care in wording her kind offer, she didn't wish to be the recipient of charity. She chafed under the knowledge that this was the only way to acquire a dress for Miriam. She pushed aside her feelings and gave Alice a warm smile. "That is very generous of you. When may we come to see the dresses?"

Before long, she and Miriam were on their way to the Colbourne's home. Cecilia grew silent as they passed the stand of trees where she had listened to nightingales with Mr. Lockhart. She wondered if she would ever experience a moment as magical as that one night. She shook off the memory. Benedict would go back to London and she would be rid of him. She was certain he would forget her as soon as he returned to his beloved city life, and it was as it should be. Mr. Lockhart would never attach himself to someone the likes of her.

"Is your family at home?" Miriam asked Alice as they arrived. Cecilia raised an eyebrow at her sister.

"Duncan is away today, but my mother is here," Alice replied.

Cecilia was grateful to learn Duncan was away. She was more than happy to avoid him, especially now that she knew of Miriam's feelings. They followed Alice up the stairs to Alice's room where her lady's maid brought out dress after dress. Miriam clasped her hands in delight. Each dress was more beautiful than the one before.

Miriam picked up a pale pink dress and held it up to her shoulders. "What about this one?"

The beaded underskirt was stunning. Cecilia was at a loss for words as she imagined the way the light would play across the dress in a ballroom. The Barnet women had never owned something so fancy. Miriam would be stunning in it.

"That is the one," Cecilia said. "It will bring out the color of your eyes and look beautiful with your hair. It's magical."

Alice studied Miriam with a critical eye. "Your figure is more delicate than mine. I'm afraid it would need alteration. And here," she pointed to the beading at the bottom of the pink underskirt, "the beads are missing."

"We have beads," the maid said. "If you are handy with a needle."

"I can do it," Cecilia said. She had never applied beads before, but she was sure she could figure it out.

"Are you certain?" Miriam asked. "I could choose a different dress."

Cecilia shook her head. "Only the best for you, Miriam," she said. "This is the dress, and I'll make sure it fits you properly and that the beading is perfect."

A smile lit up Miriam's face and Cecilia glowed inside. She hadn't seen her sister so happy since they moved here.

"Now for you," Alice said.

"No, I don't need a dress if I am not planning to attend, and I will only have time to alter one dress."

"Whyever would you not attend?" Alice asked.

Cecilia turned her back to Alice and Miriam and walked over to the window. How could she explain to Alice why she needed to withdraw from these endless social occasions?

"Was it something Mr. Lockhart did?"

"No, it's something I did," Cecilia said. "During my first season, I was exiting a carriage for a rather important society ball, and I stumbled. A gentleman passing by caught me, and it created a scandal."

Miriam rushed to her side, gripping her hand. "He was no gentleman. He swept you up and spun you around. It was not your fault, although you were the one to carry the blame."

Cecilia's cheeks were inflamed at the memory. Her ankles exposed as he spun her in the air. Her ineffective protests for him to put her down. The laughter and taunts from his friends, the whispers of the ladies behind their fans and gloved hands. And before the scandal could die down, Papa died. And the Barnets withdrew from society while they mourned. And then they had to leave their London home.

Alice took her other hand. "Dearest Cecilia, I am sorry that happened to you. What a scoundrel! Had he simply steadied you, nothing would have ever come of it. But surely you know that you have done nothing wrong."

Cecilia's mouth was dry. She licked her lips and in a voice barely above a whisper said, "I know."

And she did know. She knew she was innocent, even though the whispers and taunts and laughter followed her. During the mourning period, her friends drifted away. The young ladies her age didn't talk to her in the shops or on the streets. She'd blamed the fact that she was in mourning, but deep inside she knew she'd become the object of gossip. And she knew that it would hurt Miriam's chances.

"And when Benedict steadied you at the lake, you feared it was all happening again?" Alice asked.

"Yes," Cecilia said, remembering the warmth of Benedict's hand on her waist. "He only helped me. But I was afraid of what everyone would think. And now I can't face him, Alice. Besides, I am sure it is only a matter of time before he returns to London and we forget one another. It's best if that separation begins now. It's better if I don't attend the masquerade. No more whispers. No more gossip. If Miriam goes in this dress, she'll shine." Cecilia turned to her sister and gave her a hug. "It's your time, Miriam. I won't get in the way."

Neither Miriam nor Alice could persuade Cecilia to attend the ball. Without an appropriate dress for her to wear, they didn't dare press her too much. The Barnets gathered a small bag of beads from Alice's maid and carried the gauzy overdress and rose-colored underskirt back to the cottage. With only a few days before the masquerade, Cecilia knew it was time to get to work.

CECILIA'S NECK and shoulders ached from bending over the needle, but at last she was done. She'd finished the dress with an evening to spare. As she rose from her chair, she rolled her neck from side to side. Setting down her needle and thread, she held the dress out and inspected it closely. The extra beading had taken an extraordinary amount of time, but Miriam would be stunning in this dress. She couldn't wait for her to try it on.

Gathering the pale pink underskirt, she hurried upstairs to show Miriam. Much to her dismay, she found Miriam being helped into bed by their maid. She laid the dress aside.

"Whatever is wrong?" she asked, placing her hand on Miriam's forehead. She was warm to the touch and her face was pale.

"I'm not well," Miriam said. Her voice was hoarse and her lips were dry and cracked. Cecilia fetched her a glass of water.

"Rest," Cecilia said.

It was all ruined if Miriam could not go to the ball. She had been certain that tomorrow night under the spell of the masquerade, Miriam would meet her match and secure a future for herself. It had to happen. It simply had to. All the effort they had put into getting a dress and remaking it into something magical could not be wasted. Cecilia's fingers were pricked and rough, not fitting at all for a lady. But the dress was perfect.

"Save your strength. The ball isn't until tomorrow night. You can be well by then." But even as she said the words, she knew it was unlikely. She had not seen Miriam this ill for quite some time, and the last time she took to her bed, it had been over a week before she recovered.

Miriam cleared her throat. "You will have to go in my place, Cecilia. You will have to be me."

Cecilia let out a harsh laugh. "No one would ever mistake me for you. Never. It will have to be you. Lie still now and get some sleep. We'll talk about it tomorrow."

"How is she?" Mama asked as she entered the room.

"Not well, Mama. We must hope she recovers by tomorrow or else she will not be able to go to the ball."

Mama's face fell. "Mrs. Colbourne said this was the event of the summer, that Miriam would have the opportunity to meet several eligible men. If Miriam cannot go, it may be until next summer before she gets the chance again."

Cecilia knew many families would leave for London for the season, but the Barnets would remain here. After the season ended and people returned, there were no guarantees next summer would have any events such as this ball. The Lockharts may not summer here again, especially with Mr. Lockhart's distaste for the country.

Sadness swelled within her as Cecilia faced the reality that Benedict Lockhart would leave and return to London. She would miss their conversations.

And while Mr. Lockhart's acceptance of them had helped elevate the Barnets in the neighborhood, when he was no longer here, it would not be enough to keep them in that position. She and Miriam could very well end up languishing in obscurity. Especially after he had made a game of offending so many people. He did not seem to understand that what he thought of as playful actions had consequences for others.

"I'll have tea sent up for her," Mama said. "We must do everything to help her recover. Fetch a basin and keep a wet cloth on her head."

"Do you think it would help to send for a doctor?" Cecilia asked.

Mama shook her head. "We'll do the best we can and hope she does not worsen."

Cecilia could tell by the lines in Mama's face that she did not believe Miriam would be better.

If only she could go in Miriam's place. Although she was determined not to see Benedict again, although she did not want to risk another scandal, she wanted to give Miriam an opportunity. If only she had something to wear. A dress. Shoes. But she didn't.

"I would go, I would be you, Miriam, but no one would believe me. We are not the same size. Our hair is not the same color," Cecilia said. She looked to Miriam for support, but her sister's eyes were closed, and she had fallen into a restless sleep.

"But if you could, Cecilia, think of it," Mama said. "You will dance and meet potential suitors, but you must leave before the unmasking. When you get home, you will give her all the details and then she shall be prepared if any gentlemen come to call."

Could she pull it off? Could she be Miriam for the night?

Mama continued speaking. "You know things are precarious for us. I have not been completely honest with you about our situation. We have not been living within our means and we may not be able to stay here at Gillingham Park. We may have to seek another place—a lesser place—in which to live. If Miriam could make a good marriage, it might change things for all of us."

"Mama! How could you not tell me? I would have…." Cecilia let the sentence trail off. She would what? She had no way to increase their income. Even if she became a governess she would likely work for room and board, with a little extra money for personal expenses like her wardrobe. She would not be able to support both her mother and Miriam.

"Did Papa leave us so little?"

"You mustn't worry about it now. You must go to the ball," Mama said.

"I've nothing to wear. None of my dresses are suitable and none of Miriam's will fit me. And I have no shoes." Cecilia pinched the bridge of her nose and closed her eyes. This could not be happening. Her mind raced, trying to find a different solution.

"I'll go," she said finally. "Alice might have a dress that would work. She is not as tall as I am, but she is taller than Miriam. I'll go to Gillingham Park at once." She hoped the Colbournes would come through for her once again.

Mama gripped her arm. "You will do no such thing. It is night! Send a note with Samuels."

"Of course, Mama." Cecilia did not tell her mother that she felt safe traipsing around Gillingham Park in the dark. She could not disclose her nighttime encounter with Mr. Lockhart.

Cecilia composed a note to Alice and gave it to the butler to deliver. He was not at all happy to receive the assignment.

"Tonight, Miss?" he said, his forehead wrinkling.

"Tonight. As quickly as possible. And please wait for a reply. It is imperative that I hear back from Miss Colbourne. Do you understand?"

The older man nodded and set off. Cecilia paced the parlor but found the air stifling. She headed outside in the moonlight and wandered out onto the lawn. From here she had an unobstructed view of the drive, and she could hear the nightingales in the trees. The sky was clear tonight, and she watched the twinkling stars.

"Please," she whispered, "please let Miriam be well. Please."

When Samuels returned, he held an envelope out to her. Cecilia took it from him and opened the card.

Dear Cecilia,

I shall pray for Miriam's quick recovery. Do not fear, my friend. If Miriam is still unwell tomorrow, come to Gillingham Park in the morning. We shall make a plan. All is not lost.

Love, Alice

CHAPTER
FOURTEEN

Benedict reined in his horse. From a distance, Oakwood Manor stood, imposing and stately on the rise of ground. He was anxious for this evening, and getting in a ride this morning eased the tension. What if Cecilia had decided she wanted nothing more to do with him? He would apologize for whatever he had done at the picnic to offend her.

He hoped that she would accept his words, that things between them would be good once again. And if that were the case, he would tell her how he felt. He would tell her he wanted to spend time with her and no one else.

He was heading back to London in a few days. Oakwood Manor would be closed for the foreseeable future. While he was eager to rejoin Father, he had to admit there were things he would miss about the country, in particular, Miss Cecilia. Tonight must not be the last time he would see her. He had to find his way back here, if for no other reason than the Barnets were here. He would tell Mother that the simplicity of life here appealed to him, That it was peaceful, and a nice reprieve from the bustle of the city. Mother would be gratified to know that. She would be happy that he had come to love Oakwood Manor as she did.

The sun rose higher in the sky and he could no longer neglect his duties. Reluctantly, he nudged his horse forward and rode toward home. A flock of birds fluttered upward from a tree as he rode by, and he wondered what they were and if Cecilia would be able to identify them.

He left his horse with a stable hand and went inside the house. The housekeeper was giving direction to several maids and the butler was giving assignments to the footmen. People hustled back and forth carrying linens and candles and other necessities. He could only imagine the chaos in the kitchen as food was being prepared for the guests this evening.

"There you are!" Mother said. "Kate and I have been looking all over for you."

Oliver grabbed him around the legs. "Uncle Benedict! Will you take me riding?"

He ruffled the boy's curly head. "I'm afraid I cannot right now, but I will make it up to you tomorrow."

Oliver stuck out his lower lip in a pout reminiscent of Katherine herself at that age, which made Benedict smile. He loved his sister and her family. It lifted his spirits to be around them. One day, he hoped for a family of his own.

"Mother, there's a shortage in the delivery of the meats for tonight and...oh, Benedict! You're here," Kate said. "You may see to it while I round up my children."

"I'm sure I can sort it out," Benedict agreed. "But first I must eat. I'm famished."

"Oliver, go to the kitchen and see if there is something your uncle can eat. If he had been here earlier, he could've eaten with the rest of the family. Mother, you look tired and it's not even noon. How will you make it through the ball? You must go rest so you will be fresh this evening. Benedict and I can handle things here," Kate said.

Mrs. Lockhart agreed to rest in her room, and Benedict followed Oliver to the kitchen before Kate could give him more to do. Oliver led him to a platter of leftover bread from the morning meal. He took two pieces and offered one to his nephew.

"Why can't I come to the ball tonight?" Oliver asked.

"Have you learned the dance steps?"

Oliver solemnly shook his head. "I don't know how to dance."

"Well then," Benedict said, "perhaps you should wait until you know how to properly dance with a lady before you attend a ball."

Disappointment filled the little boy's face. Benedict slathered jam on his bread and gestured for Oliver to follow him. "I'll let you in on a little secret," he said.

Oliver trailed after him as Benedict led him upstairs and down a long hallway. A small table rested at the end of the hall. Benedict teased open a small drawer. It creaked, but finally gave way. "Go ahead," he said.

Reaching into the drawer, Oliver pulled out a key. Benedict took a bite of bread and jam and gestured to the door of the last room in the hall. His nephew fumbled with the key, but finally worked the door open. The room was windowless and dark, even in the morning hours. Oliver hung back, hesitant to enter.

"Come," Benedict said. "Put your hand on the wall and let it be your guide." He showed Oliver how to walk along the edge of the little room. When they reached the corner, Benedict had him turn and feel for a small panel with a knob set in the wall. It was as big as Benedict's hand.

"Open it," Benedict said. Oliver did and peered through the opening. The ballroom spread out below him in all of its splendor. Oliver gasped.

Benedict chuckled. "If you cannot sleep tonight, you may sneak into the room and watch the masquerade. It might even be better than being at the dance."

"Do you know how to dance?" Oliver asked.

"Yes, I do."

"I could see you dancing with a lady tonight?"

Benedict knelt by the boy and gazed out at the ballroom. "Yes. I shall be dancing tonight."

"How do you know which ladies to dance with?"

Here, in the dark room with his nephew, Benedict knew deep inside that there was only one person he wanted to ask to dance.

"I've met a lady who has become very special to me," he said. "We are…friends. And she is the one I will ask to dance." When Cecilia came, he would ask her for two dances. And perhaps they could sit near one another at dinner. The thought made his pulse quicken. He must make things right between them tonight.

Benedict's mind wandered to the garden party, to the moment when Cecilia slipped and he placed his hand around her slim waist. It had been one of the few pleasures that day. He wouldn't mind holding her in his arms. Benedict pushed the thought away and grasped Oliver's hand.

"Come on, we've got to help get things ready for the ball tonight."

"I'll be watching," Oliver said. "I want to see you dance with your lady friend. Will I get to meet her?"

"Someday soon, I hope." Benedict returned the key to the drawer, but left the room unlocked for Oliver. After he talked to Cecilia tonight, he would find a way to tell his mother he had found the woman he wanted to court. That it was one of the Barnet sisters might not make her happy, but he hoped, with time, she would come to see Cecilia as he did.

CHAPTER FIFTEEN

Alice stepped back to survey her handiwork while Cecilia self-consciously smoothed her skirt. The dress brushed the tops of her shoes. Miriam's shoes. Her toes curled away from the fabric stuffed in the toes. She hoped she'd be able to keep the shoes on during a dance, assuming, of course, that she would be asked to dance. Cecilia bit her lip and watched Alice, who was circling her, finger on her chin in a thoughtful pose.

"Well?" Cecilia asked.

"You do look beautiful in that dress," Alice said. "Even though you are taller than Miriam, I think with your hair done properly, and with the mask, you'll be able to fool most of the crowd. The dress could use something though. A bit of lace. A piece of jewelry, perhaps?"

"I have just the thing," Cecilia said. She would put Aunt Cecilia's gifts to good use. She was relieved Alice thought that she could pass as Miriam, and she would do her best to be like her sister for the evening.

Cecilia hoped she could meet an eligible young man who would be interested in Miriam. She doubted Duncan's attachment to her sister, and if she met an engaging young man at the masquerade, it would help Miriam see other possibilities.

"You will take the dress home with you. How are you going to the ball tonight?"

Cecilia realized she didn't know. "I am not certain," she said. "I'll have to ask Mama."

"If you need us to send a carriage for you, let us know," Alice said.

Cecilia slipped off the too-big shoes and changed back into her day dress. Alice carefully packed the gown into a valise for Cecilia to carry home.

"Take it out immediately when you arrive home so that it does not wrinkle," Alice said. She took Cecilia's hand and squeezed it tight. "Courage, my friend."

A lump rose in Cecilia's throat. She hadn't often experienced the kind of friendship that Alice offered. "Thank you for everything," she managed.

"Thank me later if all goes well. I daresay I will have a time of it, not disclosing your identity. I hope you are better than I am at keeping secrets.

As she walked home, Cecilia wondered if she would be able to keep up the façade of being Miriam. Mr. Colbourne would certainly know she was pretending. And maybe Mr. Lockhart. It would be best to avoid him tonight.

She didn't know what to say to him about running away from him at the pond. If she were to explain to him about the scandal in her past, it was possible he would end their friendship. She didn't think she could take that risk, yet if she did not, if she didn't repair things between them, the friendship would be over anyway. Maybe it was time to let the past be in the past. Alice was right. She had done nothing wrong, and maybe it was time for the world to know that.

• • •

CECILIA FIDGETED as she waited for Mama to come downstairs. It was time to go to the ball. The hired carriage was waiting. She paced nervously at the bottom of the staircase. Miriam's too-big shoes were not comfortable, but at least they were staying on for now. She had attached her lace from Aunt Cecilia to the neckline of the gown, and she wore the locket and blue gloves her aunt left to her. If there was ever a time she needed luck, it was tonight. She prayed Aunt Cecilia's gifts would give her the courage she needed to do what she had to do.

Mama emerged at last. She stood at the top of the stairs wearing an off-white gown that Cecilia hadn't seen since before Papa's death. A necklace graced Mama's neck, and her gloves were impeccable. All traces of mourning were gone. Cecilia didn't know what had happened to make Mama leave her drab dresses behind. To her surprise, her eyes brimmed and she dabbed at them as Mama made her way down the stairs with a grace that Cecilia envied.

"You look beautiful," Cecilia said, grasping Mama's hands.

"It is time I left mourning behind," Mama said. "I will always miss your father, but I think he would approve of us tonight. Both of us."

Maybe tonight at the ball would be a fresh start. A fresh start for Mama and Miriam, anyway. Cecilia would once more hold herself back, but this time not because Mama told her to, but because she did want to help Miriam.

"Come, our carriage awaits," Mama said.

Cecilia refrained from asking how Mama could afford it. Whatever the sacrifice was, it was worth it for tonight, even if they had to move on to a more economical place later. One magical night.

The carriage bumped and jostled down the road, but for once Cecilia didn't mind. She sat across from Mama who was gripping a handkerchief, twisting and pulling on it.

"We must leave at midnight," Mama said. "I could not afford the carriage for longer than that, and if the Lockharts follow tradition and serve the meal at midnight, we shall all be unmasked and our deception will be on display. That, I fear, would be the undoing of everything. You must stay in character as Miriam. I shall be there for you if you have any difficulties."

"Yes, Mama. I will be ready by midnight." Cecilia did not doubt that by then she would have had enough of this pretense and would be ready to leave. Besides, she hated to be away from Miriam for very long. While Miriam no longer seemed feverish and had managed to eat a bit of soup, she was still pale and bedridden.

It was not a long ride to Oakwood Manor. The house was stunning and rivaled the finest homes she'd seen in London. No wonder all of the local ladies were interested in Mr. Lockhart. The family was obviously well-off and who would not want to be the lady of such a fine home?

Cecilia stepped from the carriage without any mishaps. She followed Mama inside the manor where they were announced to Mrs. Lockhart and Benedict. Benedict frowned as she was introduced as Miss Barnet, but he did not question her and Cecilia was grateful to hide behind her mask. Other guests were arriving, and Cecilia and Mama were able to make their way to the ballroom without further trouble.

Mama squeezed her hand. "You will be wonderful tonight. I have confidence in you."

Warmth rose from her toes to her face as she accepted Mama's compliment. She didn't ever remember Mama expressing such faith in her. Not for a long time. She squared her shoulders as Papa would have had her do and followed Mama over to the Colbournes.

CHAPTER SIXTEEN

As he greeted the long line of guests, Benedict chafed under his obligations. When the Barnets came through the line and were introduced as Mrs. Barnet and Miss Barnet, he couldn't hide his disappointment at not seeing Cecilia. But then he looked at Miss Barnet and realized she was not Miriam at all. It caught him by surprise, and he failed to do anything but issue a polite greeting before the young woman that he suspected was Cecilia went inside to the ball.

He couldn't wait to find her in the ballroom, to ask her why she was in disguise. He had to admit she was rather effective at imitating some of Miss Barnet's mannerisms, but he was still certain it was Cecilia. He would know her anywhere. The shade of her hair, the tilt of her chin, the sparkle in her eyes. Other people might be fooled tonight, but he was not one of them.

The next family to be announced were Mr. Fielding, Mrs. Fielding, Miss Fielding, and Miss Daisy. Benedict hadn't spoken to the Fielding sisters since they had tried to humiliate Cecilia. He stood erect and gave them a stiff greeting. Miss Fielding seemed not to notice his lack of warmth.

"Oh, Mr. Lockhart, it is wonderful to see you again. We are grateful for the invitation this evening. I imagine it will be a wonderful ball."

He grunted in response and caught his mother raising an eyebrow at him. He shook his head, not wanting to go into detail about his previous interactions with the Fielding sisters. Thankfully, the Fieldings moved inside before they could elicit any promises of dancing this evening. He knew he was supposed to dance with as many young ladies as possible, but he only had thoughts of Cecilia.

When it came time to join the guests inside, he escorted his mother to a comfortable chair. She was all smiles and seemed to be enjoying the evening, but he did not want her to tire before the masquerade part of the evening ended. After dinner, perhaps she would retire for the evening, but for now, he wanted her to be able to enjoy the festivities.

Kate was resplendent in a light lavender gown. Her hair was curled and coiled in an elaborate style and had jewels woven through her tresses. She stood beside him and surveyed the room.

"Tell me, Benedict, which young ladies have caught your eye this evening?"

"None so far," he replied as he surveyed the room.

"You are looking for someone! Who is she?" Kate persisted.

"I am looking for the Colbournes," he said. It wasn't a lie. He did hope that if he spotted Duncan and Alice that the Barnets would be nearby.

Kate took his arm and turned him toward a cluster of young ladies. "What about one of these ladies?"

The group included the Fielding sisters. "I see nothing in that group that interests me," he said.

The first set of couples were taking their places on the dance floor as the musicians prepared to play. Miss Barnet was not among them. Good. He would have time during the first dances to locate her.

"Please excuse me," he said to Kate, extricating his arm. "I shall come back and check on Mother. I hope you enjoy the evening."

Without waiting for her response, he made his way past

the Fielding sisters and continued on across the ballroom. Cecilia had to be here and he was determined to find her. He spotted Duncan Colbourne talking to an older gentleman and made his way over to him. Benedict waited until the conversation concluded.

"Benedict, do you have a temporary reprieve from your hosting duties?" Duncan asked, clapping him on the shoulder.

"Not at all. I am now tasked with the duty of dancing."

Duncan laughed. "I'll join you. Which young ladies should we ask first?"

"Have you seen Miss Barnet?"

Duncan frowned. "I haven't. But then, I haven't seen Alice either. Perhaps if we find one we shall find the other. I will ask Miss Barnet, and you may dance with my sister."

"You wish to dance with Miss Barnet?" Benedict asked. He had noticed the two talking whenever they were at the same events.

"I do enjoy her company," Duncan said. "I see them." He nodded toward the corner of the room.

Benedict spotted Cecilia. She stood a head taller than her mother and Mrs. Colbourne.

To his surprise, Benedict was nervous to speak with her. Maybe it was better if Duncan danced with her first. It would give him a chance to speak with Alice, to ask her if Miss Cecilia harbored any ill feelings toward him.

"Mr. Lockhart," Mr. Fielding said, blocking his way. "You are not dancing?"

"Not yet," Benedict said, straining to catch a glimpse of Cecilia. She was no longer with Mrs. Colbourne and her mother. He turned to the dance floor to see her with a partner.

"My daughter would be most flattered to be your first partner."

Benedict sighed. "I would be happy to dance with Miss Fielding," he said, even though it wasn't true. He accompanied her to the dance floor, staying silent while she kept up a steady stream of inane comments. It reminded him of the last ball he attended in London, how the ladies he danced with buzzed about like swarming bees. Cecilia carried herself with a sense of calm that he found soothing. She could stand in the trees and listen for nightingales without saying a word.

The music started and he moved mechanically through the steps, circling Miss Fielding, moving toward her and back, touching hands and separating again. He kept his eye on Cecilia and her partner. As far as he could tell, they were barely conversing. Good.

"Don't you agree, Mr. Lockhart?" Rose Fielding asked.

He realized he hadn't heard a word she was saying. "Forgive me, do I agree with what?"

Miss Fielding huffed out a breath. It was childish, like Oliver. He couldn't contain his smile as he wondered if Oliver were watching the dance from the secret room.

"Mr. Lockhart!" Miss Fielding said. "Are you listening? I asked you if you thought occasions like these should be open to anyone in the neighborhood or if they should be more exclusive?"

As the music ended, he bowed to Miss Fielding. "Exclusivity is an interesting concept, Miss Fielding. My Mother invited everyone whom she believed should be included and I do not question her judgment in this matter. How do you propose she should have narrowed down the guest list? Perhaps restrict it to those with vouchers for Almack's?"

It was rude, he knew, to bring up Almack's—the exclusive establishment where the privileged were allowed access to the balls and entertainment—but he didn't care. He knew for a fact that he had never seen the Fieldings there.

Miss Fielding blanched. Good. His comment had hit its mark. Miss Fielding was insufferable, and someone needed to put her in her place. He went once again in search of Cecilia.

CHAPTER SEVENTEEN

Cecilia thanked her dance partner and left the floor. She searched for Alice or her mother but saw neither of them. A bead of sweat trickled from beneath her mask and rolled down her neck. She used the back of her gloved hand to dab at the area, then fingered the locket resting at her throat. It reminded her that she was loved, and the thought gave her comfort. She spotted Mrs. Colbourne nearby and headed toward her.

Mrs. Colbourne's mask fit over her eyes but left the rest of her friendly face unobscured. She smiled as Cecilia approached. "You looked lovely on the dance floor, my dear," she said.

Most of the people she knew here tonight were easy to recognize. Cecilia wondered once again if her ruse would be successful or if she were making a fool of herself pretending to be her sister. But many of the people here were strangers to her and she hoped that she had a good chance of making this work.

A gentleman approached them, and Mrs. Colbourne greeted him with familiarity. "Mr. Sutton, I am glad you and Mrs. Sutton could attend tonight. Might I introduce you to my new neighbor? This is Miss Barnet."

Cecilia was relieved Mrs. Colbourne hadn't introduced her as the tenant, as she might have done. She nodded to the gentleman, who was about her same height. His mask obscured his facial features but did nothing to hide the streaks of gray in his hair. His well-cut coat was made from a fine fabric and was tailored to fit his broad shoulders and slightly rounded belly.

"Miss Barnet, I am pleased to make your acquaintance. May I have this dance?"

'Yes," Cecilia agreed, managing a smile. Although this man was not a prospect for Miriam, she couldn't afford to be impolite and refuse him. Perhaps he had an eligible friend or relative that he might introduce to Miriam in the future. Mrs. Colbourne gave her an approving smile.

On her way to the dance floor, she caught a glimpse of a familiar figure. Benedict stood off to the side. She had managed to avoid him so far. He turned in her direction, but she looked away rather than risk meeting his gaze.

"Miss Barnet...Barnet...I know that name," Mr. Sutton mused. "From London? Are you related to Mr. Henry Barnet?"

Cecilia froze. What did this man know of her family? Could he have heard her name connected to the scandal? She was grateful for the mask covering her face. She struggled to control her voice.

"Yes, Mr. Sutton, Henry Barnet was my father."

"A fine gentleman, Henry. Too bad about what happened with that daughter of his." He squinted at her. "You must be the older girl. Whatever became of your younger sister? Did she find someone to make an honest woman of her, or has she become a recluse?"

She stumbled and stepped on his left foot. "I am sorry, Mr. Sutton," she said, catching her balance. Her movements were off time with the music for several beats before she regained her composure. Alice said it was a minor thing and that she shouldn't let it bother her.

"I don't recall the incident," Mr. Sutton continued. "Perhaps you could enlighten me?"

How dare he? Cecilia fumed. Her scandal had been innocent and had not marred the reputation of the man involved in the least. And now, over a year later, while discussing her late father, he dared to bring it up to her? Indignation rose within her and she refused to restrain her words. Mama would be appalled, but Cecilia was tired of letting Mama dictate her life.

"My sister, Miss Cecilia, did nothing wrong. She stumbled while exiting a carriage, and the gentleman who prevented her fall turned out to be no gentleman at all. He spun her around for sport and then stood by while his companions laughed. The London gossips chose to make that a scandal, but she was not at fault. She has no need to hide from society, but chooses to avoid the likes of you, who have nothing better to do than perpetuate rumors and sully the reputation of a young lady. Shame on you, Mr. Sutton. How dare you insult the memory of my late father in such a way?"

Cecilia was grateful for the mask which hid her cheeks, flaming with indignation. After she spoke, she thought of Miriam. Miriam's reputation. Miriam's chances here. What had she done? This man could ruin them all.

But to her surprise, her dance partner chuckled. "You are correct to reprimand me, Miss Barnet. I am too old to trifle with such gossip. I hope your sister has half your spunk. If she does, she'll weather the social storm quite well. You remind me of Mrs. Sutton." He gestured toward his wife who danced with another partner nearby. Mrs. Sutton smiled at him, her delicate mask covering the upper portion of her face.

"At midnight, when we unmask for dinner, I shall be pleased to have you make her acquaintance," Mr. Sutton said as the music ended. "Thank you for the dance."

Cecilia found herself alone on the sidelines once more. She hadn't told Mr. Sutton that she planned to be gone before the unmasking. For a moment, her deception, pretending to be Miriam, made her uncomfortable. The next time she met Mr. Sutton it would be as herself, and she'd have to pretend she'd never met him. But she was only doing it because Miriam could not be here. As long as no one discovered the truth, all would be well.

Her feet ached from dancing in shoes not meant for her, and the mask was stifling. Perhaps she could find a chair for a moment.

"Miss Barnet. May I have the next dance?"

Cecilia was startled to be asked to dance yet again. Never before had she been so popular. Was it because her face was covered? Or that people thought she was someone else?

She turned toward the familiar voice. Even with his mask, she recognized Duncan Colbourne standing to her right. She hoped that her mask was better at concealing her identity than his was.

Mr. Colbourne escorted her to a spot alongside the other couples as the music began. Cecilia moved through the step patterns toward her partner and back, trying to be as graceful as Miriam. Or as graceful as she could be in ill-fitting shoes.

"I am sorry Miss Cecilia is not in attendance tonight," Duncan said.

"Thank you, Mr. Colbourne. She was sad to miss this evening."

"Is she very ill?" The concern in his voice was genuine. She was certain that he knew she was not Miriam, and that it was Miriam who was ailing.

"She has taken to her bed with a cold, but we hope with a bit of rest that she will recover quickly."

He nodded as they touched hands and circled each other in the dance. "Please give her my wishes for her return to health."

Cecilia assured him that she would. She did not doubt his sincerity, but she was not sure what to make of his inquiry. After all, if he were promised to another, why should he be concerned with Miriam?

The dance ended and as she left the dance floor, Cecilia wished Miriam were here. The two of them could escape the warm room and retreat outside and compare dance partners. She wondered what to do next. It was proper for her to be introduced prior to accepting an offer to dance. She wondered if the rules were the same at a masquerade. If they were, she needed someone who could provide introductions. Gathering herself for more socializing, she went to find Alice.

CHAPTER EIGHTEEN

enedict watched Miss Barnet from the corner of the room. She had danced with Mr. Sutton and he'd heard her put the gentleman in his place. For a moment, he'd feared that the scene would escalate and that he would need to intervene, but Miss Barnet had handled herself admirably, and Mr. Sutton had apologized.

He knew she was Cecilia. She was too tall to be Miriam, and the candlelight was bright enough to reveal that Miss Barnet's hair was at least two shades darker than it should be. It was Cecilia Barnet at the ball. And he still needed to talk to her.

When she finished dancing with Duncan she joined Alice Colbourne. He hurried toward her before someone else could ask her to dance. It was disconcerting the way his pulse beat faster as he drew near her. Her gown showed off her figure to great advantage and he could see why she had been a popular dance partner tonight.

"Mr. Lockhart!" Alice said with delight. "How lovely to see you. Are you enjoying the ball?"

"It is a fine evening, Miss Colbourne. Would you save me a dance later? I would like to have this dance with Miss Barnet if she would oblige."

Alice squeezed Miss Barnet's hand. It was as if the two were in a conspiracy. "I'd be happy to dance with you later, Mr. Lockhart. I'll leave Miss Barnet in your care as I must find Duncan."

Miss Barnet accepted his arm and he escorted her to the

dance floor. The music began with a one-two-three beat and he shivered at the thought of taking her in his arms to waltz. It was rather progressive to have the waltz at a country ball and he wondered if she knew the steps.

He set his hand on Cecilia's waist as the music began, securing her other hand in his own. She rested her free hand delicately on his shoulder. Light, like a butterfly. He feared if he made any sudden moves, she would flit away.

"Miss Barnet," he began. "I must ask you about Miss Cecilia and what happened at the garden party. It was muddy on the shore, and she slipped. I steadied her, but I am afraid I offended her in some way. Is she still upset with me? What may I do to make amends?"

She ducked her head before answering. "It surprised her, that's all. I am sure that she has forgiven you for any perceived offense."

She looked up at him and he held her gaze. Her blue eyes searched his face. He swallowed hard.

"I've not seen Miss Cecilia this evening. Is she unwell?"

"Mir...she is indeed unwell tonight." She seemed flustered.

"That is unfortunate," he said.

She stepped on his foot as they circled to the one-two-three count.

"Please forgive me," she said. "I am unfamiliar with this dance."

"Never mind," Benedict said, "we shall learn it together."

He tried to communicate through his touch the direction she should move. As the dance progressed, their steps became better synchronized. All he could think about was having Cecilia in his arms. Dear, surprising, never-boring Cecilia.

"Have you identified any more birds at Gillingham Park?"

he asked. Surely birds would make her confess her true identity to him.

"Birds? No. You would have to ask Cecilia about that when she is feeling better. That is her interest, not mine."

"You seem…taller…this evening," he said, imagining her frowning beneath her mask.

"It is our close proximity that makes it seem so," she replied.

"If I didn't know better, I would guess that you are incognito in more ways than one this evening."

She didn't reply as he whirled her around the dance floor. He never wanted this moment to end.

"Is it true that Mr. Colbourne is promised to a young lady?" Cecilia asked.

"Duncan? Of course not. Wherever did you hear such a thing?"

"Alice told me," she said.

Benedict laughed. "That clever man. No wonder he doesn't have to fend off the ladies. He has Alice to keep them away. I have known Duncan a long time, and I can assure you that he is no more attached than I am."

The moment he said it, he wished he could take it back, for his heart was growing in attachment to Cecilia. To the woman in his arms. He had to know if she felt the same toward him, but how to approach the subject?

"Miss Barnet, do you ever miss London?" he asked.

Was it his imagination, or had she stiffened at his question?

"Not much," she said, her voice almost imperceptible above the music. "I much prefer it here. London reminds me of Papa and how much I miss him."

"Please accept my condolences on your loss. Your father was a fine man."

"Did you know him?"

"I did know him, but not well. We were acquaintances. He had a good reputation." He wanted to tell her that he remembered her. A vision in green from across the way at a ball he attended. He wanted to tell her he knew about the scandal and considered the whole matter to be foolish. It was maddening that the scandal had followed her all the way to Gillingham Park.

He must make her understand that whatever cloud she thought she was under meant nothing to him. That he was free as a swan to choose her. The Lockhart name and reputation were enough to overcome any remaining gossip about her.

He knew she was not Miriam, and never could be. Polite, polished, predictable Miriam. Gentle Miriam. A woman who was not out chasing birds across the countryside, a woman who would not have defended her family to Mr. Sutton. He had to make Cecilia understand that she was the one he wanted to share his life.

He struggled to find the words to tell her that he knew of the scandal, that he knew of her, that none of it mattered. He wanted to escort her to the best events in London. He wanted to wander the countryside discovering birds with her. It was Cecilia. Only Cecilia.

The dance drew to a close, and he gripped her hands. "May I call you Cecilia?" he asked, his voice little more than a whisper.

Cecilia pulled against him. "It is Miss Barnet," she hissed back at him. "Or Miriam."

He drew closer and she trembled. "Miss Cecilia, I know it is you. I won't give you away. But please understand me. It is you I wish to see. You I wish to dance with. You I wish to call on. Please call me Benedict, and please let me accompany you to dinner tonight. Both of us together. Unmasked.

She tugged her hands free of his. "When are you returning to London, Mr. Lockhart?"

Benedict frowned. "Very soon, I'm afraid. I will be leaving this week."

"This week?" Her voice broke. "I'm afraid I cannot accompany you to dinner, Mr. Lockhart. Our time here has been enjoyable, but I am certain it will be easy for you to put it behind you once you return to the city. Could you tell me what time it is?"

He withdrew a watch from his pocket and showed it to her. "It is almost midnight," he said. "Cecilia, I wish to…."

"Miriam!" Mother rushed toward her, her face tense. "We must go. I've received a message that your sister has taken a turn for the worse. We must leave now."

"Do you need me to send a physician?" Benedict asked, his voice filled with concern.

"No," Mrs. Barnet said. "Thank you, sir. We shall be fine, but we must go. It was a wonderful evening."

Before he could respond, a young woman interrupted them, leaving everything between him and Cecilia unresolved.

CHAPTER NINETEEN

"Why Miss Barnet, whatever are you doing here? Are you pretending to be your sister so that no one will know about your scandal in London?" The woman's voice rose above the people talking in the ballroom. With the musicians on break until after the meal, it was easy for her voice to carry.

Cecilia stopped in shock. The masked woman in front of her had a triumphant look on what Cecilia could see of her face.

"Mr. Lockhart, you should know who you are really talking to," the woman said.

Cecilia frowned as she tried to figure out who the woman was. She looked familiar. And then it dawned on her. Rose Fielding. Did Rose hate her that much? And to think, she'd once hoped the Fieldings would be her friends.

A second lady came up beside her. It had to be Daisy Fielding. Cecilia knew her cheeks flamed red beneath the mask. She had almost made it through this evening. If only she and her mother had been able to leave a few minutes ago. She should not have talked to Benedict for so long. Benedict. What was he thinking of this public display? She tried to catch his eye.

"Come," Mama said. "We must go." She pulled Cecilia's arm.

Cecilia wrested her arm free. She was tired of wearing a disguise, tired of not being herself, tired of trying to fit in and not make any trouble. She was not going to walk away now without standing up to Rose Fielding. "No, Mama. We'll leave in a moment."

She turned to the crowd. Removing her mask with trembling hands, she stood tall. "I am Cecilia Barnet. You are correct, Miss Fielding."

The woman shrank back a step and gripped her sister's hand. She did not seem to enjoy being identified.

"Yes, I know it is you, Rose Fielding. I don't know why you have sought me out and have been determined to make things miserable for me here, but this is my home. My family lives here now, and I will not apologize for it. I am Cecilia Barnet, not Miriam. Miriam is my older sister, and she is a model of propriety. I once got out of a carriage and stumbled. The man who steadied me picked me up and spun me around. It was terribly inappropriate, but it was not my fault."

She turned in a slow circle, eying the people. "Each of you may choose how you think of me. I haven't yet met many of you, but the ones of you I have met, you know me. You know I am not responsible for any scandal. I must leave now to attend to my sister, Miriam, who is ill." Her eyes locked on Benedict's. He nodded at her, and warmth flooded her.

She took Mama's arm and wound her way through the people and out of the ballroom. When they left Oakwood Manor, Cecilia was relieved to feel the cool night air on her face. She had done it. She was no longer hiding but was fully unmasked.

Mama gripped her hand with sudden urgency. "We must run," she said. "We are late for the carriage. Pray it hasn't left us."

Cecilia hurried after Mama, but the shoes hindered her. One fell off, and she stumbled forward with one bare foot.

Recovering her balance, she left the shoe behind and raced to the carriage.

To her relief, the carriage was still waiting. She and Mama climbed inside, and the coachman started the horses forward at a rapid pace. Cecilia peered out toward Oakwood Manor, clutching her mask in her hand. Was it her imagination, or was there a lone figure out on the walkway, picking up Miriam's shoe?

AS THE CARRIAGE PULLED AWAY, Mama laughed. "That is the most fun I've had in a long time. We made our getaway!"

Cecilia frowned at her. "And Miriam? Is she feeling worse?"

"No," Mama replied. "The carriage was leaving, and I needed an excuse for us to leave the ball."

Cecilia sank back in the seat, her body absorbing the jolts from the vehicle. Her thoughts flew to Mr. Lockhart. Benedict. Did he really have feelings for her? She wished she could believe him, wished that all he said was true, but doubt filled her mind. Why would he want her?

Benedict. His name rolled through her mind. She felt once again the warmth of his hand on her waist as they danced. He had known that she wasn't Miriam because he knew her. He said the scandal didn't bother him, that he wanted to court her. But the fact that he was leaving for London weighed on her.

Mama interrupted her thoughts. "I'm proud of you, Cecilia. Not for being Miriam, but for being yourself. You spoke for yourself tonight. You showed great courage."

"I am afraid I may have offended the entire neighborhood by speaking out, Mama. We may languish in obscurity."

"No," Mama said. "I saw the way Mr. Lockhart was

looking at you. It might be you instead of Miriam who marries first. That is, if you are interested in him?"

She could still feel her hand in Benedict's, feel his breath on her ear as he spoke to her during the waltz. "Yes, Mama. If he would have me, I would be interested in him. But he is leaving for London, and I think there is a very real possibility that after tonight, he'll leave me behind."

She was exhausted. Her bare foot stung from running on the rough ground. "I'm proud of you too, Mama. We did this together."

At last, the carriage turned down the long drive through Gillingham Park and rolled to a stop in front of the cottage.

"I shall help you first, Ma'am, and then you, Miss Cecilia," the maid greeted them when they were inside.

"No need," Cecilia said. "I will ready myself for bed, thank you."

The maid bobbed a curtsey and went to attend to Mama.

Moonlight streamed inside the bedroom and Cecilia didn't make a sound as she got ready for bed. She set down the mask and fumbled with the buttons on the dress. It was challenging without assistance, but eventually she was able to get the dress off. She undid her stays and let them fall to the floor. Slipping into a nightgown, she unpinned her hair. It tumbled over her shoulders.

She picked up a brush and ran it through her brown locks. Cecilia doubted she would ever fall asleep tonight after the excitement of the ball. Whatever happened now, she would forever have the memory of her waltz with Mr. Lockhart. Would she see him again? And if she did, would he still want her to call him Benedict?

Cecilia stood at the window and stared into the night. She had made it through the masquerade and she had come out of the shadows. It would take time to see if there would be repercussions for standing up to Rose Fielding, but she had no regrets. Whatever happened in the future, she would handle it as herself.

Humming softly, she held up her hand and moved in waltz steps around her room. Tomorrow did not matter. Tonight, with the moon and stars shining—tonight belonged to her.

CHAPTER TWENTY

Benedict ran after the carriage but could not reach it before it pulled away. Cecilia was gone. He was tempted to get his horse and ride after her, but he knew that Mother would want him to return to his hosting duties. Frustrated, he turned to go back inside Oakwood Manor. A tug on his pant leg stopped him.

"Uncle Benedict, does this belong to your lady friend?" Oliver stood next to him holding up a shoe.

"Whatever are you doing out of bed?"

"You said I could watch the dancing. But I wanted a closer look, so I went downstairs. Then your lady friend was running away and I followed her. She lost her shoe. I think you should give it back to her. One shoe won't do her any good."

Benedict took the shoe from Oliver and ran a finger over the embroidery. It was larger than he expected. To his surprise, he found fabric stuffed inside the toe. Perhaps the shoe didn't belong to Cecilia. He wondered if she borrowed it.

"I am not sure she will want to see me," Benedict said.

"She'll want her shoe," Oliver insisted. "One shoe is no good without the other one."

Oliver's sincere face continued to watch him. The boy was right. One shoe was useless. Shoes were meant to be in pairs, like people.

"I'll take it to her tomorrow. Come. You should get to bed before your mother finds you."

"You won't tell I ran outside after midnight, will you?" Oliver asked.

"Not tonight. But if things go as I hope, your mother will not be mad at you for helping me."

Oliver followed Benedict inside, sticking close in hopes that he would be unnoticed. Once in the house, he scampered up the stairs.

"Are you all right?" Duncan Colbourne asked. "That was quite a scene."

"Yes, I'm fine. Cecilia left." He held up the shoe. "But I plan to see her tomorrow."

"I'll go with you," Duncan said.

"There's no need."

"Yes, there is. Not for you, for me. Miss Barnet and I, well, we don't have an understanding yet, but I hope to soon. I must see if her illness is serious."

Benedict clapped Duncan on the shoulder. "When did this happen? I didn't suspect anything!"

Duncan shook his head, almost sheepish. "We have talked on several occasions. And danced. I find her most appealing, and I believe she would be the perfect wife for me."

"Yes, she will be the perfect wife for a country gentleman," Benedict agreed. Duncan was a fine man, and if he married Miriam, her future would be secure.

"Congratulations," Benedict said. "I believe the two of you will be very happy. Do you plan to speak to her mother?"

"Tomorrow," Duncan said.

"I'd be happy to have you accompany me to the Barnet's home tomorrow. I wish to speak to Mrs. Barnet myself."

"You've lost the wager, then?"

Benedict was a bit embarrassed to admit it. "I'm afraid so."

"And will your parents approve?"

"If Mother believes Miss Cecilia is responsible for my

new fondness for the country and Oakwood Manor, I am sure she will agree. She says she only wishes for me to find happiness."

When Benedict re-entered Oakwood Manor, he found the guests had been directed to the dining room. Several long tables had been joined end-to-end to form one long line. Servants were already bringing in food. He gave the shoe to a footman and asked him to take it to his room. It was important to keep it safe until he could return it. Mother raised a questioning eyebrow at him as he took his seat at the head of the table. He nodded his head in what he hoped was a reassuring gesture.

He barely tasted the food and found it hard to make conversation. His thoughts were on Cecilia. She'd been incredibly brave to unmask herself and stand up to the annoying Fieldings. The ladies were seated halfway down the table from him. He wished they'd been escorted away from the property, but he only had to endure them for a few more hours. He suspected they would not be following him around and clamoring for attention the rest of the night.

The woman to his left asked a harmless question and he struggled to come up with an appropriate answer. The evening couldn't end soon enough for him. Somehow, he made it through the meal and back to the dance floor where he danced with several of the older married ladies from the neighborhood. He'd always found the custom of spouses not dancing with one another to be odd, but tonight he was grateful for it. It was easier to lose himself in the company of his mother's friends than to feign interest in the young ladies closer to his own age.

At long last, as the new day dawned, the remaining guests departed, and he went wearily to his own quarters. He longed to sleep and gave his man instructions to wake him in a few hours. Sending the servant away, he pulled off his boots, loosened his cravat, and stretched out on the bed. As he closed his eyes to drift off to sleep, he imagined he was dancing a waltz.

CHAPTER
TWENTY-ONE

Cecilia stifled a yawn. She had slept late, as had Miriam and her mother. Miriam was better this morning, and Cecilia sat in her room as her sister had toast and tea. She told Miriam about Mr. Sutton and the Fielding sisters.

"I cannot believe the Fieldings were so unkind to you," Miriam said.

"Yes, in front of everyone. But I took off my mask and told the entire ballroom the truth about the scandal. It is all behind us now, even if we are shunned in society forever."

"I should think we will not be shunned. It took great courage for you to do that." Miriam settled back against her pillows.

"Enough about those wicked girls, Sissy. Tell me again how you waltzed with Mr. Lockhart," she said, her eyes shining.

It was gratifying to see Miriam feeling better. "I was clumsy. I even stepped on his foot, but he had his hand on my waist and directed me through the steps, and eventually I was able to follow him and sail around the room."

"Are you glad you went?"

Cecilia paused. Was she glad? The dance with Benedict had been like a dream come true. And she was happy that she stood up for herself at the ball. But things might be complicated in the neighborhood now, and with Benedict heading to London, she feared the future would not be happy for any of them. Still, she did not wish to upset Miriam while she was recovering.

"Yes, I am indeed glad that I went, although I missed you terribly. I am sorry that you were not able to attend."

Miriam peered down at the breakfast tray and took another sip of tea. "I shall hope that my opportunity comes sooner rather than later. You deserved a night out, even if you had to pretend to be me."

"You should have seen Mama, out of her mourning clothes. She was beautiful last night." Cecilia proceeded to entertain Miriam with descriptions of gowns and a list of the people she'd met. It pleased her to see Miriam eat while Cecilia talked.

When Miriam finished, Cecilia offered to take the tray downstairs rather than wait for the maid. "You rest now, sister, and I shall bring my embroidery this afternoon and keep you company."

Cecilia delivered the tray to the kitchen and went to find Mama. When she approached the parlor, she heard voices inside. Male voices. Her stomach flopped like a fish out of water. Who was Mama talking to? She didn't dare hope that Benedict had come. It was probably an older gentleman come to either chastise her or court her. Neither option appealed to her.

She hesitated before entering the parlor. To her surprise, Mama was speaking with Benedict and Mr. Colbourne. Mr. Colbourne's cheeks were flushed a bright red, but he smiled at her when she entered the room. Benedict bowed. "Miss Cecilia," he said.

"What a pleasant surprise to see you," she said as Mama invited them all to sit. Cecilia glanced at her plain brown dress and wished she had paid a little more attention to her appearance. She reached up to her hair and tried to smooth it. Mama frowned at her and shook her head. Cecilia dropped her hand on her lap.

She hadn't expected to see Benedict again, certainly not here in the cottage. His presence drew her like a magnetic force, and she fought the urge to stare at him. Unbidden, the memory of his hand on her waist as they danced filled her thoughts.

"Mr. Lockhart brought back Miriam's shoe," Mama said, holding it up.

"Miriam will be grateful, I am sure."

"Were you with her just now?" Mr. Colbourne asked, his eyes anxious.

"Yes, she is feeling much better this morning. I suspect she'll be good as new tomorrow," Cecilia said.

The room lapsed into an uncomfortable silence and Cecilia wondered what she was meant to do now. She'd always found visits to be awkward, and she missed Miriam's presence more than ever. Benedict cleared his throat, and she raised her chin to face him. His eyes caught hold of hers and she startled at the intensity of his gaze.

"Miss Cecilia, will you do me the pleasure of showing me around the grounds?" he asked, his voice low and husky.

Cecilia turned to her mother and to her great surprise, Mama nodded. "You may accompany Mr. Lockhart, dear. But you must not be out too long."

Thankfully, Mama did not tell her to wear her bonnet as if she were a child. She hid her surprise that Mama would let her out in the company of Mr. Lockhart but stood up and excused herself from Mr. Colbourne. The maid brought her bonnet, and Cecilia tied it in place. Once outside, Mr. Lockhart offered her his arm.

She glanced back at the house, fighting her old fear of scandals, before placing her hand at the crook of his elbow. He guided her into the small garden where roses and foxglove bloomed. Overhead, birds called. She raised her head to see two swans flying across the blue sky. She wondered where they were headed. Perhaps to the lake where she'd seen them before.

Benedict grasped her hands, turning her toward him. "Swans, Cecilia," he said. "Do you remember how we said they stay with one partner for life? I want you for my partner. I want you to be the person who I accompany through life. I love you. Only you. From the first time we met, it has always been you. Marry me. Let's fly together. Say you'll be my wife."

Cecilia's eyes burned and a lump formed in her throat. Benedict Lockhart wanted to marry her. And she wanted to marry him.

She bit her lower lip. "Are you returning to London? Because my home is here. My place is here."

"If you'll have me, I'll stay here as long as you'd like. While we would have to spend some time in London, our home could be here, at Oakwood Manor."

He was staying. Her heart leapt up in her throat and words failed her. He waited for her answer.

"What of my mother and my sister?" she asked, forcing out the question through dry lips. As much as she wanted Benedict, she worried about her family.

"I have it on good authority that Duncan intends to ask your sister to marry him. Between all of us, your mother will always have a place. Say yes, Cecilia. Let's make our own decisions like those swans. Say you'll have me, and we can speak to the vicar about the banns and be wed in a few weeks."

Cecilia nodded as one of the tears brimming in her eyes spilled over and rolled down her cheek.

"You're crying," he said, reaching up a thumb to wipe her tear. "Don't cry, dear Cecilia. Have I upset you?"

"They are happy tears, Benedict. I never dreamed that you would love someone like me. Yes, I will marry you."

"Then you have made me the happiest man in England." He bent toward her and pressed his lips gently on hers. She wrapped her arms around his neck and kissed him back while his arms encircled her waist. He kissed her again before releasing her.

"Come, let's go tell your mother the news."

"Mama! What if she doesn't approve?" Cecilia said. "What if your mother doesn't approve?"

"Your mother already agreed, and my mother was impressed with *you* last night. I have assured her that you are the woman I respect and admire. She wants us to be happy."

With that, Cecilia took his arm once again and they went back inside.

ecilia followed Benedict out into the moonlit night. Oakwood Manor was quiet and there was a chill in the air. He clasped her hand, entwining his fingers with hers. She gathered her skirt with her free hand and they ran toward the trees. Benedict stopped her at the edge of the grove, placing his hands on her waist and lifting her from the ground. He spun her around and set her, laughing, back on the grass. Benedict cupped her face in his hands and bent to kiss her. As he did, a nightingale sang.

"Did you hear that?" she asked.

"Yes, I did," he said, speaking softly near her ear. "Nightingales sing here at Oakwood Manor as well as they did at Gillingham Park." The heat of his breath on her skin made her shiver.

This time when he moved to kiss her, she met his lips with hers. He pulled her close.

Cecilia loved how her body fit against his, as if they were made to be together. She ran her fingers through his unruly hair and clasped her hands behind his neck. He was starlight and birdsong and fresh air all rolled up into one, and she couldn't believe that he was hers and that she was his.

"We mustn't stay out too late," she said, breaking away from his kiss.

"Why not, Mrs. Lockhart?"

Cecilia smiled. She would never get tired of him calling her that. Their wedding had been simple, and perfect, and all she ever wanted.

"Because, Mr. Lockhart, we mustn't be tired for the wedding tomorrow."

He rested his face on her shoulder. "I am sure that Duncan and Miriam are quite capable of getting married without us."

She laughed. "Of course they are, but I would never miss the wedding of my beloved sister, and I promised Mama I would arrive on time."

Benedict placed a finger under her chin and tilted her face up to his. "We must keep those promises, and then I shall sweep you back to Oakwood Manor where we will refuse all social engagements for at least another week." There was a growl in his voice that made Cecilia's spine tingle. A week alone with Benedict would be magical indeed. She still wanted to pinch herself each morning since their wedding to make sure that it was all real.

"But we must invite Mama for dinner at least once. I cannot leave her all alone in the cottage once Miriam gets married."

Benedict kissed her soundly. "One week, wife. Your mother will understand. Perhaps she will visit with Duncan's mother. Then we shall invite her to live here at Oakwood Manor. There is plenty of room, and when Mother comes to visit, they shall have each other for company."

"One week," Cecilia promised. "But no matter how long we are married, we must always have this. Nights alone under the stars listening to the birds."

He smoothed her hair back from her face. "Always and forever," he said.

"And happily ever after," she replied as he bent to kiss her again.

AUTHOR'S NOTE

Dear Reader,

We are far enough removed from the Regency era that it sometimes seems like a fairy tale; an era of grand estates, lavish balls, and strict societal structure. It was a natural fit to set a fairy tale retelling in the Regency era, and when I got the invitation to create a novella as part of a multi-author series, I jumped at the chance.

Why Cinderella? As I read various stories searching for one that resonated with me, I realized I always loved the story of a down-on-her-luck heroine with a hero who sees her worth. I knew from the beginning that the story would have a shoe and a ball. In the Grimm version, the stepsisters maim their feet to make the shoe fit. I decided to turn that upside down and have the shoe NOT fit Cecilia, my Cinderella character. And what Cinderella story would be complete without a ball? During my research, I realized a masquerade was the perfect event to include in my Cinderella retelling. Many of my characters wore masks in a figurative sense throughout the story, and they needed to shed those masks to be true to themselves.

By the time I finished writing, I had incorporated a loving family, two "mean girl" characters, and one fairy godmother. While there is not a magic system in my novella, the historical era provided a magic all its own. I tried to write with historical accuracy, but my work is imperfect. Any mistakes in historical representation are mine.

Creating books requires both a writer and a reader. What you bring to the story is as important as anything I have written. Between us, we create something beautiful. Thank you for reading this novella. Any time you read a book, recommend it, review it, or request it from your local library, you are supporting an author. THANK YOU! Books do not happen without the support of readers, and I am so grateful for readers everywhere.

I love hearing from readers, and you can connect with me through my website: www.amynewbold.com.

Let me know what you loved about this story!

Happy reading!

Amy

ACKNOWLEDGMENTS

I am honored to participate in this multi-author project with the following talented writers: Audrey Glenn, Sienna Peake, Amanda Panhorst, Jenni Ward, Mary-Celeste Ricks, and Heloise C. Kensington. If you have not already done so, consider reading their books!

A special thank you to Jenni Ward for her amazing cover illustrations and design work.

It takes a village to create a book.

Thanks first and foremost to my family. **Greg, Josie, Daniel** and **Will**, you are my biggest cheerleaders, and I could not do it without you. Thanks for all the encouragement, meals, cleaning, laughter, and more. **Shannon** and **Maren**, thank you for being so positive and supportive about this project.

To my beta readers and critique partners:

Sierra Wilson – Thank you for inviting me to participate in this project and for answering all of my questions. When I wasn't sure if I would make any deadlines, you made accommodations that let me finish the project, and I am so grateful. You make me a better writer.

Michelle Henrie – Thank you for helping me develop the plot when I was stuck. You are not only a fabulous writer and mentor, but also a valued friend.

Daniel – Thank you for being willing to read everything I write. I appreciate your thoughtful insights and your willingness to discuss last-minute changes.

Greg – You kept me going in so many ways. You are my

first reader and are always willing to listen. Thanks for getting me through these past few months. This book does not exist without you.

Josie – Thank you for helping me see ways to make a Cinderella story have positive family relationships, and for helping lay the groundwork for this novella. You were always available for a late-night plot brainstorm.

Will – If you hadn't written a novel during your sophomore year of high school, I never would have tried. But you told me I could, and I did. Thank you for sharing your beautiful writing with me.

Holly Perkins – Thank you for reading my story! The parts of the story that resonated with you are even better now and thank you for telling me Duncan and Miriam needed more. You were right!

And finally:

Thanks to my dad who taught me how to read and who always took me to the library.

Thanks to my mom whose love of books and reading is contagious. How blessed I am to be your daughter.

Thanks to my sisters who were writers long before I was. Your examples and support made this possible. Jodean, you are the steady influence in my life. Lark, you are the best writing partner anyone could ask for—I can't wait to write with you again.

To all of my fellow writers: you are inspiring, and when I grow up, I want to be like you.

ABOUT THE AUTHOR

Amy has always loved fairy tales, history, art, and reading. She grew up making snowmen during Utah winters and learned to read at age four. She wrote her first monster story in elementary school and her favorite dinosaur is a stegosaurus. Hiking, camping, birding, and spending time in nature help fuel her creativity. Amy is an avid board game player and has a deep appreciation for chocolate. She loves to travel and to spend time with family. When not traveling with her spouse, illustrator Greg Newbold, Amy enjoys exploring the world through books.

OTHER BOOKS IN THE SERIES

Read all the books in this captivating series, mixing the charm of the Regency period with the magic of fairy tales

A Lady Most Engaged by Audrey Glenn

Inspired by Sleeping Beauty

A compromising situation at Rosedale Castle leaves Harriet Thornhill unexpectedly engaged to its enigmatic earl. Bram, Lord Rosedale, is captivated by his unexpected fiancée, but courting her proves challenging between his manipulative mother and flailing estate. In a world of duty and expectations, can Harriet and Bram write their own fairy tale ending?

A Lady Most Fitting by Sienna Peake

Inspired by The Elves and the Shoemaker

Charlotte Linfield wants nothing more than to please her exacting father and prepare for a perfect London season. Getting tangled up with the teasing young gentleman from the local shoe shop is the last thing on her mind.

Philip Notley is just after a bit of fun when he begins leaving secret gifts for the new girl in town. What starts as a prank soon proves something far deeper, but will it be enough to bring two mismatched halves into a perfect pair?

A Lady Most Untamed by Amanda Panhorst

Inspired by The Brother and Sister

Arthur Fairhurst is a terrible duke. Jumpy and nervous around others, he prefers hiding away in his Northumberland forest collecting, sketching, and researching all the wildlife he can find to satiate his inexhaustible curiosity.

Mara Boswell, a lone gypsy, excels at making herself invisible. Her longing for a home and someone to love of her own is nothing compared to her desire to keep herself safe. When Arthur, dressed as a plain gameskeeper, finds her, they are both surprised by the cautious friendship that blooms. But can a duke really love a gypsy?

A Lady Most Intrigued by Jenni Ward

Inspired by The Frog Prince

Amidst the clattering looms of Lancashire, a forbidden love blooms...

Hannah Sheppard yearns for more than the expectations of society. John Ingham dreams of a life beyond working at a mill. A late night rescue brings them together, but a family secret may tear them apart forever. Can their love survive the secrets of the past, or will the truth shatter their hopes and dreams?

A Lady Most Entangled by Mary-Celeste Ricks

Inspired by Rumpelstiltskin

Rupert Stilson can never resist a damsel in distress. When Charlotte Dawson becomes entangled in a plot to rob her father of his daughter and his estate in one fell swoop, Rupert rushes in with flax and loom to save the day. But the danger is hardly over once the wager is won. If Rupert cannot trust Charlotte with the secret of his real identity, her family will never truly be safe.

A Lady Most Isolated by Heloise C. Kensington

Inspired by Rapunzel

Hidden away in a tower by her guardian, Arabella Stewart longs for a chance to experience society and find friendship. Sent to the Dorsetshire coast at his uncle's behest, Charles Fairfax is happy to avoid London's matrimonial traps until the discovery of a maiden in a tower makes him reconsider his reluctance to marry. Is he courageous enough to rescue this lady? Or will disapproval and deceit destroy their hopes?